Seventeen-year-old Mariam
supernatural since she was ;
Beast showing up in her da
years old and the fact that she can't die, it doesn't come as
too much of a shock when drought-ridden Los Angeles
turns into a sentient, carnivorous rainforest overnight.

The tedium of wandering through a ruined city filled with
dead bodies and crumbling buildings is broken when she
stumbles upon beautiful Camila and her ragtag crew of
survivors. Mariam isn't exactly altruist of the year, but
her soft spot for kids means she can't just leave them to
fend for their own. She rescues them and decides to throw
her lot in with theirs.

Despite herself, she quickly becomes a part of their family.
However, even as they all start feeling at home in their
new vegetal world, sinister figures from Mariam's past
begin to reappear, and the whole hell-jungle situation
begins to feel a lot more personal. As she learns more
about her family's involvement with the unnatural forces
that caused all of this destruction, Mariam is faced with a
terrifying truth: she might have to betray someone to save
the city and her new friends.

UNDERGROWTH

Chel Hylott and Chelsea Lim

A NineStar Press Publication

Published by NineStar Press
P.O. Box 91792,
Albuquerque, New Mexico, 87199 USA.
www.ninestarpress.com

Undergrowth

Printed in the USA
First Edition
December, 2019

Print ISBN: 978-1-951057-97-8

Also available in eBook, ISBN: 978-1-951057-96-1

Warning: This book contains non-consensually involving a child in a contract, mentions of suicide, death of a parent, alcohol use by a parent, graphic violence, and gore.

Chapter One

THE DOOR GIVES way with a wet squish, and Mariam wrinkles her nose against the smell. Damp wood, ripe fruit, the sharp tang of tree sap, and, yup, there it is: there's something dead in here. Probably whoever thought holing up in a hardware store would save them. At least, she thinks it's a hardware store. The sign out front is mossed over in green, and the display window has been overrun with vines. Still, it seems like the right kind of place.

Mariam doesn't really want to go inside. She's seen plenty of death, and the smell is rank enough, it's almost certain that there's more than one body in there. But she's here for a reason, and who knows when she'll next get another opportunity this good? She needs tools, and there are tools here.

Shoving a shoulder against the door gets it open wide enough to slip through. Inside, it takes a minute for her eyes to adjust, but eventually, rows and rows of shelving swim up out of the darkness. Everything is slick with damp.

Under the death, there is the smell that is particular to home improvement and hardware stores, something like sawdust and varnish. That and the nails scattered all over the floor indicate she's found the right place. She bends to pick up one of the nails, considers it, grabs a box off the shelf, and stuffs it into her backpack. Who knows? Maybe she'll need them at some point.

Down the first aisle, then. Screws, nuts, hex bolts...halfway down she trips and catches herself, but not before something moist brushes her ankle. She looks down and sees a leg, then another. Bile rises to her throat; she chokes, the stench suddenly overwhelming, before she steadies herself, hand on a shelf. Memories of her mother rise before her, short blonde hair streaked with red and gray slime, sprawled over the floor, her pale white hand blackened with gunpowder. Then Mariam blinks, and she's back in the dark, the stink of blood replaced with that of rot, and nothing to be heard but the *thudthudthud* of her heart.

A family, maybe. Those shoes are too small for an adult. She leaves them where they lie.

She tries to distract herself and rakes her eyes over the shelves in a direction away from the bodies, and a large red toolbox catches her attention. She walks over and tries to open it. It's stuck fast. She tries not to think about the bodies, thinks instead of her father, and braces herself, then pounds the toolbox with her fist. Her flesh breaks and she hisses, but as soon as the pain hits, it shifts a register, run through with a tingle of the supernatural. Skin knits back together before her eyes, and she bites back the scream that's welling up inside of her throat. Goddamnit. If she could turn it off, she would, though that might not be advisable in her current situation. It's useful, she can't deny it, but the pain feels like more trouble than it's worth.

At least the toolbox is open now, and the pain's cleared her head. She takes a shaky breath as the scar fades away into clear skin and peers inside the toolbox.

Inside she finds pliers, a pair of shears, a utility knife, two screwdrivers, and a chisel. She puts them into her backpack and moves on to the next aisle, where a shelf of flashlights piques her interest. Promising. But when she finds the batteries to go along with them, they're all wet and leaking acid. So much for that.

Three aisles later and she's picked up a coil of nylon rope and a dust mask, but what she really wants is at the back of the store. A rack of sledgehammers, picks, and axes has fallen over in the corner, already half overgrown with slippery vegetation. Mariam lifts one after another, testing them for weight and grip and something else she can't pinpoint.

The last one is wedged under the rack itself, but she yanks it out and blinks at it in the dark. This one. This one will do. It's small, just a little hatchet with a wooden handle and a blade painted red, but it feels heavy and solid in her hand.

She gives it a couple of practice swings and smiles to herself as it snicks through the air. It'll cut through the less robust vegetation, in any case, and it's still light enough to use as a weapon if she ever needs it. And she probably will, if she's honest, despite the twist it puts in her gut. There are animals, now, smarter and more vicious than they have any reason to be, and plants, too, that will grab at your ankles and wind themselves around your neck if you aren't careful. And there are people. Not many, it seems, but there are some, and Mariam knows people aren't always friendly in times like these.

The hatchet sits snug at her hip, looped through her belt.

She avoids the first aisle and its inhabitants on her way out. A careful step over the vines at the door and she's back out into the perpetual gloom of what used to be a six-lane boulevard. It's morning still, probably. Overhead, the arms of newly sprouted trees make a lattice of dripping green that just about blocks out the sky. Down here on the ground, time passes almost imperceptibly, everything slow and sluggish like she's underwater with only faint, filtered light from on high to guess at the position of the sun. Maybe time stopped when the tremors ceased. Maybe a lot of things.

It's been weeks, now. How many, she's not exactly sure. For a while, she'd kept track of the days in a little notebook, but then a curious vine plucked her pen right out of her hand, so that was that. And what's the point anyway? By now she's pretty sure humans won't be around long enough to read anything she writes for it to matter, not if what happened here happened everywhere.

It started with the blackouts, which wasn't so bad. Just another summer storm rumbling through, making the lights flicker with its static, she'd thought. But soon there were rolling waves of vibration that pulsed through the walls, through the floors and ceilings, and set her bones to shuddering. The lights brightened, dimmed, buzzed, and then popped. When they went out for the last time, who was to know they'd never come back on?

After that it was quiet for the space of about five seconds. All the electric humming in the whole world suddenly gone. It was the kind of stillness no one had known for a hundred years or more.

Then, a sound like a screech, like the earth itself was screaming. The sky flashed neon and the ground shook and shook and shook. Suddenly in her nose, the choking stench of smoke, sickly sweet but caustic all the same.

She doesn't know, really, what happened next, because she was home alone at the time, and, yeah, she'd locked herself in the basement with a box of crackers and three bottles of water until it was over. A couple of times someone had banged at the door, and once they'd begged and pleaded, but she didn't open up. She's not ashamed. It kept her alive, which is more than can be said for most people who ventured out to help their neighbors or investigate or whatever the hell they were doing outside. She's found their bodies all over the place. Some of them still had skin.

The bodies aren't the main feature, though, because most of them are gone by this point, overgrown or threaded through with leaves or sunken into the peat. The world is different now.

After the last of the aftershocks faded, she'd crept up to the door and peered outside to discover that overnight, everything had turned green.

So much for the drought. So much for ripping out your lawn and replacing it with desert plants, because, oh man, this is not a desert anymore. Los Angeles is now a clot of humidity and vegetation. Huge trees, their trunks furred with moss, sunk their roots right through what used to be highways and sidewalks and stretched up to tangle their branches in the windows of skyscrapers. Every surface, it seems, is covered with flat, spongy leaves or snake-like vines that secrete a sticky sap when they get agitated.

It burns, the sap. Mariam found that out the first time she tried to fend them off and came away with her palms crisscrossed in acid burns. They healed up quick, like they always do, with painful side effects, and she's been careful ever since.

The vines aren't the only things to look out for, and in the short time she's been out here on her own, she's discovered that pretty much anything can turn out to be deadly. Not long after she'd crawled out from her house, some guy she knew from around the neighborhood called to her from across the way and started toward her, until halfway there, he shrieked and the ground just swallowed him. She didn't go over to investigate. That's the kind of stupidity she has no time for.

She doesn't quite know what to do after raiding the hardware store. Without a purpose, the emptiness that's threatened to eat away at her since she was a tiny girl hovers at her consciousness, so she does what she usually does when despair sits heavy in her gut. She goes to the ocean.

She used to spend so many nights at the beach, playing her guitar for strangers and staring at the sky. It was her place to think. Maybe it can still be.

It turns out to be a bad idea.

Finding it at all is hard enough with her sense of direction torn to shreds from all the new vegetation. The vines mostly leave her alone, but every so often, like a curious kitten, they bat at her face, hair, and clothes. It's disconcerting and horrible and weird. The vines cease their explorations once she removes her hatchet and starts swinging wildly, anger and a case of the heebie-jeebies giving her newfound strength. At first, sap stings at her face and arms, but that will pass. Better than to have the creepy things all over her.

She gets close to the beach when her heart stops.

She can hear people, lots of them, and dogs barking too, somewhere on the other side of a thick lattice made of branches and vines. Through the chinks in the trees, she can see them moving, bright spots of color in the green.

She yells, "Hey! In here!" and jogs as fast as she can through the tangled plant life toward the voices.

"Hey!" she shouts again as she gets closer, but there's no answering call from the other side of the vines and no change in their movements. Mariam peers through a gap in the vegetation, just a little gap as wide as her hand. She can tell it's almost sunset, but even so, it's blindingly bright out, the sun bouncing off the ocean, and she has to squint for a moment before things become clear. Closer to her, a group of men and dogs are milling around on the beach: military, probably, based on their uniforms. One's talking into a radio, the rest walking back and forth along the tree line, peering in suspiciously.

"Hello? I'm in here!" she calls out again, but even to her it sounds muffled, and none of them turn.

"No, can't get through. Chainsaw didn't even leave a mark—the stuff just kept growing back thicker. We're going to head out," the man on the radio says, and his handset crackles in response.

"No way through the top, either. Wait, there's something going on. Something's moving down there, it's...looks like vines. Vines are..." There's a pause, and the static buzzes louder, then, "Oh my God, they're coming at us! They're pulling us down! Someone help! Someone—" The radio crackles again, this time ominously, and Mariam hears a crash somewhere far behind her. She curses under her breath.

What the hell is going on?

She tries another, "I'm in here!" as loud as she can, the desperate sound scraping at her throat, but it's obvious they can't hear her. They don't even turn. Instead, they shuffle nervously in place and glance around at one another in silence before their leader puts the radio to his mouth and asks, "John? You there?"

Static.

After another moment the man issues an order and they turn away, dogs and all, heading back toward the sea.

"Wait!" Mariam cries, but they're already climbing into their boat. Someone starts the motor.

She has to fight back tears of frustration and anger.

Mariam scrubs an agitated hand through her hair, cropped close to her head but still longer than she likes—she'd been due for a haircut already when disaster struck. Now it's threatening to tickle her ears and stick to the back of her neck.

What's she gonna do now? Hack her way through to the beach to try to get to the people there? She can't. The vines are too thick and her little hatchet isn't big enough. If the military with all their tools can't get through, how can she even begin to—

She hears a shriek inland. Sounds like one of those scary smart monkeys. She'd better get away from here before...another ungodly scream rents the air, and wait. That doesn't sound like a monkey.

That sounds like a little girl.

Mariam hears more shrieks, childish voices screaming in horror, adult voices shouting to run. She looks at her hatchet, and her eyes harden. Then she runs back into the overgrowth, her weapon at the ready.

Chapter Two

THE DENSE FOLIAGE cowers before her hatchet, peeling back like a curtain to reveal a scene from a nightmare. There's a young girl lying on the carpet of moss, her throat bitten open and leaking blood, her brown eyes frozen in a blank stare. Gray furred bodies zip through the air, shrieking and bloodthirsty. One of them grabs another girl rushing toward the dead kid, and that's where Mariam steps in.

She raises the hatchet high and brings it down on the monkey's head, quiet and efficient. Hot blood splatters her face. Some of the viscous liquid gets into her mouth. It coats her tongue with a bitter metallic tang, and she spits it out, raising her hatchet again.

"Go!" she tells the girl as another monkey flings itself toward them, and she hacks into the animal's neck.

After that, there's a flurry of violence as the monkeys re-evaluate and assess Mariam as the threat. They come at her all at once, and although their claws and teeth rip into her skin, she bites her tongue at the pain and ignores it as best she can.

She misses a swing and suddenly there's a furry whirlwind in her face, knocking her back onto the ground. The moss catches her, soft, and she rolls to dislodge the monkey, but its little hands scrabble at her face, claws raking searing grooves into her cheeks, her forehead. Then as quick as it came, it's gone with a squawk, and there are two heavy boots planted on the moss next to her head.

It's a man, just a dark silhouette in the dim glow of the canopy. Mariam takes his offered hand and scrambles up, reaching for her hatchet where it's fallen in the brush. When she wipes a hand over her face to get the blood out of her eyes, her fingers find her cheeks already smooth and tingling as the last of the scratches fade away.

The monkeys are in retreat now, swooping away through the trees and chattering angrily to one another.

Mariam turns to calculate the damage.

Just one human body, but the one is far too young. The rest of the kids are huddled near the largest tree trunk, behind a woman standing like she's still ready for battle. She's holding the littlest, who shares her straight, dark hair and whose cheeks are streaked with tears and dirt. Scattered belongings dot the clearing like so much colorful debris.

Mariam makes a chopping motion in the air with her hand and addresses the group.

"You need to move. Get out of here before they come back with more friends. Take your food, and leave anything else that might weigh you down. Go."

The woman's eyes widen and her jaw works for a second before she can speak. "But, Nayara—the girl, her body. We need to bury her," she finally gasps in softly accented English, still clutching at the little girl in her arms like she's afraid the child will float away.

"I'm sorry, no time. Go, and I'll cover your backs," Mariam says again, sparing just the flicker of a glance for the child's corpse.

"She's right," the man rumbles from behind her. "Take the food packs and get moving. But I'll do the covering. You—" He turns to Mariam. "—will you lead them?"

She nods, despite that she doesn't really want to get tangled up with this group and their ragtag act. They don't look like they'll last long.

Mariam takes a moment to squint up at the sky—which way was the beach? Maybe those men will come back—though to be honest, she doubts it. The sky is almost dark now, and through the tree's overhead, it's impossible to tell which way is which. No help, then. Mariam turns in what she thinks might be the right direction.

"Okay, follow me," she says.

They do, forming a straggling line behind her as she sets out through the tangle of trees and plants, swinging her hatchet in front of her to hack through the thinner obstacles. It's almost too dark to see, but, as Mariam's learned over the past few weeks, once night falls, some of the spongier vegetation takes on an eerie, greenish glow. It's convenient if a little creepy. She brushes her hand along a glowing leaf and comes away with phosphorescent dust coating her fingertips.

They've been stumbling through the almost-dark in relative silence—the littlest one is still sniffling—for at least two hours with no sign of the beach before Mariam admits to herself that they're hopelessly turned around. They might as well stop and rest. She holds out her arm to halt the group, and they gather around, tired and solemn.

"We can stop here, yeah? It's getting late, and we're far enough away from your original campsite now."

The woman nods.

More to break the silence than anything, Mariam says, "What did you do to attract the monkeys' attention? We need to know so we can avoid it next time." She winces at her use of the word "we" as the others come in closer around her.

When still no one answers, she pushes. "Was it the fire? Was it—"

A girl about Mariam's age with long dark hair down to her hips and a tired expression makes a noise, then falls silent. The rest of the kids shuffle their feet and the smallest boy, a brown-skinned kid with brown hair, stares at the little girl clinging to the woman's hand.

The long-haired girl speaks. "Someone found a baby monkey and brought it to camp. Before we knew what was happening, Nayara was screaming and screaming..." She pauses and shakes her head. "And they were going so fast and they just..." Her voice breaks into a sob. The little boy hugs her leg.

"It was Hana," he declares, lifting his little nose in the air and meeting Mariam's gaze as he pats the long-haired girl's leg in an effort to reassure her. "She's the one who brought the monkey back."

The little girl holding the woman's hand gives a cry, her little face turning red as she begins to wail. The woman, who Mariam assumes is related to her in some way, clutches her closer, her features schooled into impassivity. The little girl squirms away and then crouches on the ground, rocking back and forth as she cries.

"The fancy man gave it to me! He said it would be my friend!" It doesn't make any sense, but the little girl obviously believes what she is saying. Mariam chalks it up to the child's imagination.

She's tiny, this one, maybe four years old, if that. Mariam can just see it, this titchy child with her face split wide open in a smile, and probably a little monkey with a grin to match, and, no, Mariam does not consider herself a smooshy kind of girl, but there's nothing she can do about the way her heart melts for the kid.

"No, no, I'm sure she didn't mean—it's okay, it's—" She reaches out but the girl recoils, so she steps back. "It's not your fault. You didn't mean it. We know that. It's not your fault, it's not. Right, everybody?"

The woman nods, and the long-haired girl detaches herself from the boy to kneel beside the tiny girl and comfort her. A round, dark-skinned girl with tight ringlets nods as well, but her heart doesn't seem to be in it. Mariam can't help but notice a resemblance between this girl and the one they left behind but shakes the thought.

"It was a mistake anyone could make," Mariam offers.

She waits a few minutes and lets the little girl cry herself out. When the woman—her mother maybe? sister?—picks her up, Mariam nods.

"Yeah, we'd, uh, better make camp here." She begins to sit down and tries not to think about those blank brown eyes, and then blank blue ones.

LATER, WHEN EVERYONE is fed and most of the blood has been scrubbed off Mariam's face, the woman, whom the others call Eun-Ji, introduces her properly to the group.

There's Ishmael, friendly of face and outfitted with a shotgun, his black skin shining in the light of the fire. He seems like a gentle, sensible sort of man, despite the gun, and Mariam can't help but like him right away. He has a prosthetic leg that he removes when he joins them, sighing in relief. He smiles when he's introduced.

Luci is the girl who bears a resemblance to Nayara, and who probably would have been dead herself if not for Mariam's hatchet. She tries not to think about it, but the phantom taste of blood still lingers in her mouth. From what Mariam's gathered, Nayara was Luci's little sister. Poor kid. She's just sitting there trying not to cry and refusing to eat. That's gotta be tough.

Camila is the long-haired girl, maybe just a year or two younger than Mariam, and Carlos is the boy who clings to her pant leg. His round glasses keep slipping down his sharp little nose.

The littlest one is named Hana. She's stopped sniffling now but only eats when Camila insists her hair will fall out if she doesn't.

Then there's Eun-Ji herself. Eun-Ji is the de facto leader, Hana's mother, and Carlos's foster mom. She's young, can't be too much older than Mariam, but she's a lot tougher than her willowy appearance would suggest, and the kids listen to her without protest.

They won't risk a fire despite the dark, but Mariam taps a tune against her thigh and stays up once the others have all gone to sleep. She's staring at a glowing leaf, trying not to think about how she's going to leave these people without them noticing, when Eun-Ji stands, cradling Hana against her breast.

She drops a hand to Mariam's head and suggests, "Maybe it's time for you to go to bed, too, hmm? We have a lot of scavenging to do tomorrow, and you'll need your strength."

Mariam nods and rests against a mossy log. Hygiene went to hell when the rest of the world did, and she doesn't mind the dirt in her hair the way she would've before all this.

The last thought she has before sleep claims her is that she could get used to falling asleep with the gentle sounds of their breathing and snores around her. It doesn't bother her as much as it should.

WHEN SHE WAKES in the morning, only Hana and Carlos are still there, Hana curled not too far away and sucking her thumb. She can hear the others' voices through the trees behind her, murmuring softly. Nice of them to trust her with the kids, she supposes, and she watches for a second as Hana rolls over in her sleep. Even in the weak morning light, her face glows with a kind of innocence that kindles a strange warmth in Mariam's chest.

Yeah, she might be stuck with these folks. All the altruism she hasn't felt since the quakes started wells back up in her chest. There's no abandoning them now, anyway, not the way she's gotten herself tangled up in their rescue.

She stands and stretches, makes sure Hana and Carlos are still soundly asleep, then takes a few steps toward the voices. She doesn't have to go far before she catches sight of them, crouched down at the base of a tree with smooth, papery bark the color of tea. Ishmael has his arm wrapped around an expressionless Luci. Camila rocks on her heels a little ways away, and Eun-Ji—Mariam stretches up on her toes to see—Eun-Ji is kneeling on the tree's roots, carving something into the trunk.

"There," Eun-Ji's saying as she lowers her little knife, a waver in her soft voice. "Now she'll be here forever." She sits back and Mariam gets a look at what she's done: a name carved into the tree bark, crude but neat: Nayara. That kid. That little kid.

Camila's shoulders shake and Eun-Ji reaches over to lean their heads together. Mariam turns away. She can't help them with this—she doesn't know yet how to handle her own ghosts, never mind theirs. But there are other things she can do.

She doesn't stray far because Hana and Carlos are still asleep at the camp, but she slips her hatchet into her belt and walks a ways until she finds what she's looking for, a tree with bright yellow fruits dangling at head level from thin, swinging branches. She plucks a few of the fruit, gathers an armful of it, and heads back to camp, where she dumps the pile on the ground and flops down next to it.

The thing about most nonpoisonous plants in this god-forsaken forest is that they're covered in thorns and spikes and they're near impossible to get to without getting hurt. These are no exception. Mariam, however, is uniquely suited to this task.

The fruit looks like a cross between a cactus and a pinecone, and Mariam knows from experience that the flesh tastes kind of like passion fruit seeds and apple. It's weird, but it's edible and sweet and probably one of the more nutritious things around here.

She's peeling the fruit when a shadow appears over her. It's Eun-Ji.

"Hi."

"Hello."

"Um...you okay?

"Yes. I had a question for you," Eun-Ji ventures.

"Shoot."

"Ishmael said, and I know this sounds crazy, but he said you can heal yourself? Like...magic?"

Mariam stops peeling the fruit and then looks up at Eun-Ji, who is shorter than Mariam, but from Mariam's position on the ground, the older woman seems like a giant, and she seems suspicious.

"Yes."

"How?"

Mariam shrugs. "I don't know. It started with the earthquakes." That's a lie if ever there was one. Mariam's been able to heal since she was six, but Eun-Ji is a stranger, even if she is nice, and Mariam doesn't quite know if she can trust her yet. Besides, this lie is easier to swallow than the truth.

"I guess I shouldn't be so surprised," Eun-Ji says. "Anything can happen if this can." She gestures around to the trees, now towering above them, that popped up almost overnight just a few weeks ago.

"Thank you for helping us," Eun-Ji continues. "Not everyone is so generous anymore."

Mariam shrugs. What can she say? That she's still thinking about leaving them because she's not sure they'll survive the next attack? Best not.

"No worries. I'm glad I could help."

Eun-Ji nods uncertainly. "Right. Anyways, I'll be with the children. If you need any help with those, just let us know."

Mariam agrees and breathes a sigh of relief when Eun-Ji leaves.

Chapter Three

BY THE TIME she's almost done with the fruit, it must be getting close to noon, because the light filtering down from above is shining just a smidge brighter, casting dappled shadows over her hands. The pattern gets her thinking about baby deer, of all things. Probably something to do with all the nature shows she'd watched when she was a kid with her mom before...before she lost her mom. It's funny the little things she remembers from her childhood. Even though she was young, there is a clear before and after. Before, Mom trying her best to replicate Mariam's grandmother's molokhiya for dad's birthday, to Teta and Ammu's delight and surprise. After, sullen Ramadan night meals alone with Dad, maybe a phone call to the family if he wasn't too busy dabbling with the occult. Mariam shakes her head to dispel the thought and looks up as the brush rustles and something approaches. She thinks it'll be a vine or Eun-Ji, maybe even Ishmael, but no, it's that Camila girl.

"Hey. Eun-Ji said you might need help?" Camila offers, her hands splayed before her like she's approaching a wild animal. Well. She did see Mariam go all berserker on those monkeys. For all Mariam knows, that's exactly what everyone thinks of her. She shouldn't mind but finds she does. She shakes the thought away. Hopefully, the adults haven't told any of the kids about Mariam's healing.

"I'm almost finished, actually." Mariam shrugs, affecting nonchalance because up close, this girl is pretty cute. She hadn't gotten a good look at her before, what with the attacking and the fleeing and the darkness, but in the somewhat light of day, Mariam can't help but notice. Okay, fine, like really cute. Her long hair shines in the dim light, which is a feat, and her smile, friendly despite whatever wariness she must be feeling, is bright against her brown skin. Mariam feels herself flush. But right now isn't the best time to be developing a crush on anyone, and Camila probably isn't interested anyway

"You sure?" Camila makes a noncommittal gesture, and Mariam sees the reflection of the dull light on the metal of Camila's knife.

Mariam rubs her hand through her hair and motions next to herself. Camila sits down crisscross and picks up a fruit. Mariam doesn't laugh when the other girl winces at the prick of the thorns, and instead pretends she didn't see it.

They work in silence for a while, piling up fruit between them, before Camila asks, "Where'd you learn to fight like that? I mean, it was pretty impressive."

"Nowhere. I kinda swung and got lucky, I guess." No way she's telling the pretty girl she's a freak if the others haven't told her yet. Hah. Not going to happen.

Camila looks at her with some mix of disbelief and disdain. "There's not a scratch on you and you expect me to believe it was dumb luck?"

Oh, thank God, she doesn't know. "Believe what you want, princess. Doesn't matter to me," Mariam bristles.

Camila's tch of annoyance is cut off when she pricks her finger again and sticks it in her mouth to suck away the bubble of blood.

THE GROUP SOMEHOW makes its way around them an hour later, Hana bouncing excitedly for more fruit and climbing all over Camila.

"Careful," Mariam cautions Hana. "Camila's using a knife and you might get—"

Ishmael swoops in and picks Hana up, throwing her up into the air. "S'okay, Mariam. I got it. Wait, sweetheart. You've had, like, three already! Luci's only had one."

"Fine," Hana grumbles, but there's still a giggle in the corner of her smile.

Mariam stares at them with amusement and curiosity. She wonders how all these people met. Did they know each other before the quakes? Did they just wander around LA and find each other in the chaos of the jungle? It's bizarre. What's even weirder is that she feels so comfortable with them already, as though she's known them for a lot longer than the twenty-four hours or so since she stumbled into their lives. They just have something about them, this feeling of family she and her father never really had after everything that happened.

Everything that's happened. Oh, *oh*! Mariam shoots up and hurries to Eun-Ji and Ishmael.

"I actually have some idea of what's going on," she says. "With the whole forest thing. It's not everywhere. I was down at the beach before I ran into you guys, and..." She notices Camila staring at her, and Luci, too. The little ones don't seem to be paying attention, and while Mariam had hoped she could have this conversation in private, it's more important that the conversation happens at all. Besides, they all have a right to know, don't they?

"There was military down at the beach, outside the forest. Soldiers, dogs, maybe a helicopter. They were looking for survivors, I think. They couldn't come in, though, couldn't even hear me shouting even though I was right there."

"What do you mean?" Eun-Ji asks.

"It was like...there was a wall. I know it sounds impossible, but it was like an invisible wall. I just couldn't reach them, and they left before I could do anything. So, that sucks. And maybe we're stuck in some kind of bizarre force-field jungle dome..." She trails off at the looks on their faces, then shrugs and tries to put a happy spin on it. "...but, I mean, at least the forest isn't a worldwide thing like I thought it was. It looks like it's not even the whole US, not if the military is still functioning. They have radios, and helicopters, and technology that works. There might be a way out of here."

Eun-Ji and Ishmael exchange a glance, and Mariam sees the disbelief, and also a little despair, pass between them before they look back at her.

"We've been thinking about that ourselves," Ishmael says slowly. "Our original plan was to head for the ocean, but if what you're saying is true...maybe we should go north, into the hills. It could be cooler up there, and if nothing else, we might be able to get a better view across the city."

Mariam nods. "Seems like as good a plan as any. I've been wandering around the west-side, mostly, but I haven't found much." She doesn't mention the things she has seen: the moss-wreathed bodies, the fresher ones that seemed to have dropped dead moments before she came upon them. Surely this group has found them too, and they don't need reminding of how dangerous everything is now. But still, she has to ask, "Can you guys, I mean...it's tough going in the forest, and with kids..."

"They go as fast as they can, but we have to stop often," Eun-Ji says. "To be honest we haven't made it very far in the past three weeks."

Three weeks? Mariam checks this against her internal sense of time and is unsure. Surely it can't have been that long already? If she's counting the days, though—and she's sure someone as fastidious as Eun-Ji is—it seems about right.

"Well, we'll do what we can, then," Mariam says eventually. "But it wouldn't be smart to stay in one place. We've got to try to find help." She pauses abruptly, suddenly aware of how much she's presumed about her membership in their little family. "That is, I mean, if you want me to go with you. I could always..." Her voice peters out then; blood rushes to her face.

"No, we totally want you on our side. You're a wonder with that hatchet," Ishmael says. He quirks an eyebrow at her, at once amused and serious.

Camila's been quiet all this time, but she speaks up now, a frown starting between her eyebrows. "What if we can't get out?" she asks. "What if it's like Mariam said, all around, and no one can hear us, and we're just stuck in this forest forever, and...and..."

Ishmael puts a hand on her shoulder. "We won't know unless we try."

Eun-Ji clears her throat. "Ishmael and I had better go scavenging for some blankets and clothes in the houses nearby. Could you and Camila please watch the kids?"

Luci grumbles that she's "not a kid" and Eun-Ji smiles.

"I can go instead," Camila says, her voice lowering so only Eun-Ji and Ishmael and Mariam can hear. "I mean, you should probably spend some time with Hana and Luci is still a bit... I just think it'd be a good idea for Luci to have you two around." Eun-Ji's face takes on a contemplative expression, and after a few moments, she nods.

"That's fine. Would you mind going with her, Mariam? We don't want any of you going off by yourselves. It's not so safe." Worry laces through Eun-Ji's features as her eyes dart off in between the trees. She's right; who knows what's out there?

Mariam nods and stands. "No problem, Eun-Ji."

MOST OF THE buildings Mariam has seen are like this: half-collapsed and overgrown with foliage, liable to fall the rest of the way down with the slightest encouragement. The earthquakes did most of the damage, probably, and what they left behind is being slowly eaten by green and roots and rot.

Mariam goes in first, stepping carefully through the gap in the door where it's hanging off its hinges. Inside, everything is quiet and still—the leafy vines coating the walls don't even have the insidious tremble of their outdoor brethren. The floorboards creak under her foot, but the ground holds steady, so she pushes the door a little wider and motions Camila in behind her.

"Watch your feet," Mariam says, pushing aside a clump of moss with the toe of her shoe. Camila might have nodded, but Mariam isn't looking, instead advancing forward into what must have been a living room once. The ceiling is warped and buckled, courtesy of the earthquakes, and a mass of dark, bulbous fruits with smooth skin have made their home in its fissures. They're a little creepy, probably poisonous, and Mariam ducks her head to avoid them as she makes her way around the room.

Camila pulls off a quilt draped over a lumpy sofa. The air that wafts toward Mariam smells damp, and maybe even a little moldy, but they can't really afford to be picky. Into the backpack it goes. There doesn't seem to be much else salvageable, though, so they move on to the kitchen— or, they try to, but just past the doorway the linoleum slopes down alarmingly and the narrow room ends in a confusion of crushed wood and tiles.

"Let's...not go in there," Camila says quietly over Mariam's shoulder. And yeah, Mariam has to agree, even though she'd really been hoping to find something canned and delicious. This all-fruit-all-the-time diet is getting old, fast.

"Uh-huh, good call." She steps back and loses her balance on the uneven floor and bumps into Camila, who reaches out to steady her.

"You okay?" Camila asks.

"Yeah. Thanks."

There's another room just down the hall, maybe a study or something similar. Mariam gives it a pass and goes on to the bathroom, but Camila lingers at the door, and when Mariam gets back with an armful of towels, she's inside, kneeling in front of a lopsided bookcase.

"What are you doing?" Mariam is annoyed without really knowing why. She leans against the doorframe and hugs the towels close to her chest in lieu of crossing her arms.

"I... I thought it'd be nice if we had books we could read the kids. I left my only one back where Nayara— where the attack happened," Camila says.

"You're joking. We need to get food, Camila. Supplies. We don't have space for books."

"Books are important." There's a stubborn set to the line of her jaw, and her hand moves to rest possessively on top of the books she's already picked out.

"Yeah, maybe when you're not trying to survive the apocalypse. Leave them. We don't have time for this."

"I'm taking them."

"You're not."

"Are you seriously saying that a couple of books are going to make a difference in our packs?" Camila's face is red with anger.

Mariam sighs, frustrated, but Camila has a point, and Mariam doesn't really want to fight. "Fine. Choose one. We need to prioritize food."

Camila's mouth opens as if to argue, but then she nods and hesitates over the books. Eventually, she chooses one, a slim green volume whose cover looks vaguely familiar to Mariam, and stands.

"Okay, let's go."

Off to their left, the hallway leads to a staircase, somehow mostly intact despite the damage to the rest of the house. When Mariam tests her weight on the first step, it neither creaks nor collapses, which seems like a good sign. Pictures line the wall on the way up, and though the frames are cracked and fogged over with humidity, the faces are still there. Kids in front of a Christmas tree, a dog, a boy in a baseball cap. Mariam glances over her shoulder and sees Camila peering at a family portrait: mom, dad, kids.

"Come on, I want to get back before it's too late," Mariam says, and Camila almost jumps.

"Sorry, yeah. Go on."

They're almost to the top when a step emits a *scree* and jagged darkness swallows Mariam's foot. She shrieks and reaches out to grab the railing, but the wood detaches from the wall, trailing tendrils of vine, and sends her falling backward.

Camila catches her, and they both tumble down until Camila lands on her back with a hand to break their fall and cries out.

When Mariam finally disentangles herself from Camila, she growls, the stress of the day having gotten the better of her. "What do you think you were doing?"

Camila winces, holding her right hand in her left. "I think I hurt my wrist. A thank you would be nice. You know, I did catch you."

"You hurt yourself." A bubble of panic grows in Mariam's belly. She doesn't know when she became so invested in these people's lives, but a handicap like a sprained or broken wrist? It could heal wrong. It could make it difficult to climb if they need to; hell, what if her hand hadn't been there! What if Camila had hurt more than her wrist?

"Are you absolutely insane? What were you thinking?"

Camila shakes her head, not understanding. "Um. I was behind you? I wasn't just going to let you fall and break your neck on the stairs."

"It doesn't matter, I would've been fine! Now we have to deal with this, and—"

"What are you talking about? Hello? A broken neck is not fine!" Camila interrupts.

"I..." A lie almost passes between Mariam's lips, but she realizes that she can't get out of telling, not after her outburst. She's going to have to tell the pretty girl she's a freak after all. Mariam tries to think of a way to explain, but after a minute of silence and Camila's confused stare, Mariam mumbles, "Dammit." Didn't Ammu always say doing is more powerful than saying?

She bites the inside of her cheek and smacks the back of her hand into the corner of the wall. There's a crack and a crunch, and ow, ow, ow, she probably could have done that a little less dramatically, but when she holds up her crooked pinky for Camila to see, it's already popping back into place. Again, ow.

Camila just freezes, still cradling her own wrist and staring at Mariam with an open mouth. Finally, it snaps shut and then opens again, for Camila to say, slowly, "I'm sorry, what? What the hell just happened? And, are you okay?"

Mariam waves her hand, whole with all its intact fingers splayed, in front of Camila's face. "Like I said: fine. I can't die. I can't get hurt. Don't ask me how, or why, because I don't know." Well. That's not exactly the truth or even close, but telling Camila that her dad literally made a deal with the devil and now Mariam can't stay hurt? It's a little too early for that. She wants the girl to like her, after all. "This is just me," she finishes, then pauses and takes a breath to chase away the last of her irritation.

She really can't be mad at Camila for being shocked. God knows she herself had freaked out the first time, when her scraped knee just up and knit itself back together after she'd fallen off her bike at six years old.

Camila mutters, mostly to herself, "Well. I guess it's not the weirdest thing to happen in the last few weeks."

"That's the spirit. Now—" Mariam holds out her hand—the other one—to Camila. "—let's take a look at your wrist before we check out the other houses."

BY THE TIME they've made their way through the neighborhood, Mariam's shirt is missing a long swatch of fabric from the bottom half, exposing her belly. The fabric wraps around Camila's wrist as a makeshift bandage.

The backpacks they're wearing are bursting with canned goods and clothes; Mariam's even managed to snatch a can opener out of one of the kitchens. They have blankets, which Mariam is carrying, and a first aid kit. There was a pot Mariam had wanted to grab, but Camila made the point that they could cook things in the cans, and a pot would only weigh them down.

As they start back toward the camp, Camila asks quietly, "So that's how you didn't get hurt with the monkeys, huh? The whole regeneration thing. Must be pretty useful."

Mariam shrugs. "I guess."

"It doesn't hurt? I mean. At all?"

She sighs, annoyed. This is why she doesn't tell people. Ishmael and Eun-Ji at least have the tact not to pry.

"A little? It passes. Hey, can you not, you know, tell the kids? It'd probably freak them out."

"Yeah, of course." Camila's eyebrows furrow. "Wait. Do Eun-Ji and Ishmael know?"

"They figured it out."

"After the attack."

"Yeah."

Camila opens her mouth to ask another question, then seems to decide against it. She just rubs the skin above her wrist and keeps picking her way through the knotted vines at her feet.

A little later, when they've almost made it back to camp, Mariam slows and looks over her shoulder. "Hey, Camila?"

"Mhm?"

"Thanks."

A wrinkle forms above Camila's nose. "For what?" she asks.

"For trying to save me, even if it was really stupid of you."

Camila laughs.

Chapter Four

LATER THAT NIGHT, Mariam notices Luci sitting away from the fireside, her fingers twiddling with the edge of her shirt. Her face is dirty, like all of them, but there are the faint tracks of tears smudged on her cheeks, too, and Mariam knows Luci hasn't been eating much since the attack. She's heard Eun-Ji and Ishmael arguing in hushed tones about whether or not they should just leave her be. Ishmael thinks they need to let her process things, but Eun-Ji argues she needs to keep eating.

"Nayara was all she had left. I'd probably be acting up worse than Luci if I was in her place."

"But she needs to eat! I can't lose her, too, Ishmael! I can't!"

The conversation had dissolved into little hitching sobs and a rumbling murmur after that, and Mariam had moved away to give the two of them some space.

She doesn't feel bad about the eavesdropping, though. She likes these people, but she doesn't know them well. Better to know what's going on than to stay in the dark. She learned that with daddy dearest.

"Hey. Mind if I sit here?" Mariam asks, pointing to an empty space of log.

Luci shrugs. "If you want." There's a hitch in her breath like she's trying not to cry.

Mariam perches beside her on the log and rests her chin on her hands. She lets the silence rest between them until Luci's small gasps turn into controlled breathing.

"So, how'd you all meet each other?" Mariam asks once she's sure Luci can talk.

Luci shrugs again. "Carlos and I are both foster kids. After the quakes stopped, Eun-Ji and Ishmael went to check on us—me and Nayara. Camila was with us, babysitting, 'cause Rob and Dave, my foster dads, they, uh. They were out when everything started, so...they never came back." She lets out a long, wobbly sigh, and then starts crying again.

Mariam doesn't really know what the best course of action is, so she just sits there in silent support. Sometimes all you need is a good cry, and she remembers all the times her Ammu scooped her up into his arms and let her go at it until she couldn't cry anymore. Mariam can't scoop Luci up, and even if she could, she doubts Luci would appreciate it, but being there is something she can do.

"Everyone's dying," Luci finally says after the tears have subsided. "Everyone."

Mariam glances at her and looks back at the fire. "People do that. But you're not dead."

"I wish I was." Luci looks sullen, pulling on a curl. "I wish I wasn't alone."

"Hey." Mariam is sympathetic, really, but Luci's not alone. "Eun-Ji and Ishmael are worried sick about you."

"But they're not...everyone has someone! Eun-Ji and Ishmael have each other. Carlos has Camila, and Hana has her mom, her real mom. And I'm just me, and no one wants me. All the people who loved me most are dead and I didn't even get to say goodbye!" Tears gush from her eyes once more.

Mariam considers. Not one of them has asked, yet, about where she came from or how she ended up wandering through the rainforest all by herself, and she appreciates that. It's nice to just be, helping gather the food and carry the packs and sing the kids to sleep, without having to explain herself. Now, though, seems like it might be a good time to say something.

She sighs out between her teeth. "I lost people, too. Pretty much everyone, actually. It sucks. But you know what? You keep living. You keep living because that's what they'd want for you. You keep living because that's what people do. We survive."

Luci shrugs, gives an angry little sigh of her own. "What do you know? It's not like you've ever survived the apocalypse before either."

Well, Mariam can't argue with that. She pats Luci's knee and stands. "Hang in there, kid."

AFTER SHE'S HELPED Ishmael dispose of the empty cans far enough away from the camp to keep any animals from getting too curious, Mariam heads back to the fireside. Eun-Ji's made her a pile of blankets, not far from where Camila's set up her own bed.

Mariam waves a hello and Camila nods around a squirming bundle that turns out to be Hana, who's sitting in her lap while Camila runs a salvaged brush through her hair. It catches on the tangles that are inevitable when you're living as a refugee from the apocalypse, but Hana doesn't mind. She's just humming as she plays with the strands of Camila's hair that are falling over her shoulder.

"Your hair is pretty," Hana says, twisting a brown lock in her stubby fingers.

"Thanks, I like your hair a lot, too," Camila says and runs the brush down the back of Hana's head again. Hana shivers and hums, and her eyes close for a second. Then they snap open again and she twists around in Camila's lap, a grin spreading across her face.

"Your turn!" she exclaims, grabbing at the brush.

"I'm not done with yours yet, silly," Camila says, but she's laughing and lowering her head so Hana can trace the brush over her scalp. It must feel nice, because Camila closes her eyes too, letting Hana tease out the knots until they're all gone. And Hana is right, Mariam can't help but notice: Camila's hair is pretty.

Mariam decides she wants in on this. She stops before them, hands resting on her cocked hip.

"Hey, will you brush my hair too?" She leans down and Hana reaches up, giggling, to run the brush through Mariam's overgrown pixie cut. Camila is smiling as well, her cheeks flushed just a little, and for a minute Mariam forgets she's not really a part of this little group. For a minute, Mariam feels like she belongs.

The minute passes, and Mariam shudders. She doesn't know why, but there's a strange feeling, as if something is watching her. She tries to ignore it, but even as Hana pulls the brush through her hair, she can't seem to shake it.

The feeling follows her to bed, but so does Camila, after Eun-Ji appears to carry a sleepy Hana away. Camila crouches nearby and starts to plait her hair as Mariam slides into her nest of bark and blankets.

Camila doesn't say anything, so eventually Mariam quirks an eyebrow and asks, "Yeah?" The feeling of being watched has left her skin prickling, and more anxious than she's used to, so she's feeling a bit antsy with Camila looking at her like that.

"You're really good with Hana," she finally says.

"She's a cute kid. What's not to like?"

"Yeah, that's true. Um. I just wanted to say thank you. I don't know what we would've done without you and your hatchet. I mean, I don't know how we would even be here. And you're so good with the kids, and—and you know so much about, like, fruit and foraging and stuff, and—I guess—what I'm trying to say is—I think you're cool. We should, I dunno. Maybe we should hang out when the world isn't ending. I mean, if it ever stops being like this. You could—teach me? Like all the stuff you know?"

Where did that come from? Mariam feels a flush rising in her face and she does her best not to splutter, or laugh. She doesn't know why she wants to laugh. Not that she's complaining. She thinks Camila is pretty cool, too, and who is she to turn down a laundry list of compliments from this girl?

"Oh, um, thanks. You...too? And uh, yeah. We should totally hang out, but like, we can do that anyways. Like, now? Or tomorrow. That's good too," she finally manages.

"Great!" Camila says, a little too loud.

The silence stretches between them, and Camila looks like she about to stand when Mariam says, "Hey. Mind if I ask a question?"

Camila shrugs. "Sure, I mean, of course."

"I was talking to Luci, and she said you were babysitting. Is that how you know everyone?"

"Yeah. I've been babysitting them all for a long time, so they're like family."

"What happened? I mean, to your family. What happened to them?"

Camila's normally open and cheerful face closes off then, her brown eyes shutting against the sudden shine in them.

"Um, uh. I don't really know. I think—I think they

didn't make it. Uh, I don't wanna talk about this anymore. See you tomorrow. G'night," she says, then stands abruptly and gets into her own bed, turning her back away from Mariam.

First Interlude

MALIK WINCES, SHIFTING uncomfortably from his position in the tree. He's been here for hours now, watching, his suit dusted with a whole evening's worth of dead plant matter that's sifted down from the canopy above him. He brushes it off his knee absently and squints down at the darkened camp below. His eyesight is better than ever now, even in this unnatural gloom, and he examines each of the restless piles of blanket in turn. Mostly children; mostly helpless, he thinks. What on earth is Mariam doing wasting her time with these people? She needs to hide, to survive. She had the right sort of idea when she was trying to get out, but then, that was never going to work: this place is designed to keep things in.

He shakes his head. Whatever anyone might say of him, no one can say he isn't a devoted father. Even if his child is particularly headstrong and defiant. It is rather poetic, her saving a group of people he directly put in danger, in more ways than one. If he were the man he was eleven years ago, his heart would be brimming with pride for her selflessness, but he is not that man and has not been since Alexandra's suicide. And why should he be? The book and the Beast...each have given him more than anyone else could have. Of course, his brother Aamir hadn't approved of his new isolationist tendencies, and sure, perhaps Mariam should have seen her grandparents and cousins more often. But he did it to save her. To save the both of them. Forever.

But he much preferred when Mariam ignored her neighbors in lieu of pursuing her own survival.

It is so much easier for him to look after one person than it is seven. His ridiculous daughter is going to get attached to them. Clearly, she's already attached to one particular member of the group. It was almost painful, listening to that. But this propensity for attaching herself to things, like the puppy she'd pet-sitted for a week, like Aamir before he moved away, is going to hurt her in the end. He's going to have to break her of that bad habit, but for now...maybe, for now, he'll let her do what she wants. As long as her survival isn't at risk, he supposes making an alliance with these people can't hurt her. It's going to make protecting her so much more troublesome, sure, but he always liked a challenge, and besides, he's so well equipped for this kind of thing now.

Well. As long as that girl's crush doesn't get in Mariam's way. If it does, he might have to kill her himself to spare them all the indignity of teenage puppy love.

Malik smiles, his face stretched unnaturally wide, and uses the most recently acquired of his abilities. His body shrinks down, his limbs retreat, and his tongue forks. His snake form shimmers in the dull light as he winds his way down the tree and slithers to the ground.

Chapter Five

THE STUDY DOOR wavers into existence before her and she reaches for the doorknob above her head, because this scene is familiar: she's six years old, just back from lunch with Uncle Aamir, and she's looking for her mama. The knob turns; the door swings open on silent hinges.

There it is, right where she expects it: the blood on the carpet, the dull sheen of the spent gun, her mother's body splayed on the floor. The only sound in the room is the tick of the clock on the wall. Mariam makes to leave, to run to her father and into his arms, but now, of course, now her mother stirs, and she's rising, sitting up, and, and,

"Mama?"

She's turning, and Mariam rushes to her because she was dead—she was gone—and now she's here.

But instead of her mama's perfume, the stench of rotting fruit fills her nostrils, choking and thick. Mariam's fingers tangle in her mother's hair and come away coated in a fungal slime.

And her mother turns.

She turns.

Hers is the face of a thousand monsters, all hanging skin and empty eyes and a gaping mouth crawling with flies and maggots. A terrible mask of human skulls adorns her head because she isn't herself. She's the Beast. She's always the Beast.

Its voice is a chorus of horrors as It laughs, and Mariam screams.

She wakes with a gasp and the sensation of bugs skittering over her skin and scalp. Camila is there, leaning over her and shaking her shoulder gently.

The soft light filtering through the trees suggests the sun is already up. She blinks blearily.

"Mariam, Mariam, wake up, you're dreaming," Camila's saying through the haze, and it takes Mariam a second to clear the buzzing in her ears before she can respond. Even then, it comes out as a sleep-inflected jumble.

"I...Wha?"

"You were having a nightmare, I think. Are you okay?" Camila sits back on her heels and glances behind her, and that's when Mariam realizes Camila isn't the only one staring at her with a mixture of confusion and concern. She's the center of attention, apparently. Carlos blinks at her from behind his glasses, wide-eyed and curious. Luci gives her a weird sideways stare, and even the unflappable Ishmael seems a little unnerved. Only Eun-Ji isn't looking, and Mariam is pretty sure that's because she's trying not to.

Yikes.

She huffs and sits up in her blankets, running a hand through her hair, sweaty and hot even by rainforest standards.

"I'm fine. Thanks," she says, loud enough for everyone to hear.

It works because Eun-Ji sends the others a meaningful look and they conspicuously return to their various tasks, leaving Mariam and Camila alone by the remnants of last night's fire.

"Do you...want to talk about it?" Camila asks, tentative like she expects Mariam to bite or flee, and, huh, maybe she will.

"Not a chance in hell, sweetheart." She smiles sharply before shrugging off her blankets and standing. She snatches her hatchet up off the ground from where it laid beside her in the night and swings it up over her shoulder.

"Be back later." Mariam waggles her fingers and then strides off into the brush.

HALF A MILE from camp, Mariam stumbles over a particularly thick vine and gives it a vicious kick for its impudence. When it rears up to retaliate, she cleaves it in two with her hatchet. Her breath comes hard, and she scratches at the hair that's prickling her neck.

Stupid. She hacks at a nearby tree trunk.

Stupid. She hacks at it again.

Stupid that she still has these dreams. Again, and this time a good wedge-shaped chunk of wood goes flying.

Stupid that they can still affect her like this.

Another.

Stupid that her first instinct is still to call for Ammu so he can talk her back to sleep.

Her hatchet drops to the ground with a *thunk*.

Ammu, Uncle Amir, who abandoned her just when her dad got really weird. Okay, maybe that's unfair. He got married, and his wife had a lucrative career on the East Coast, so of course, he had to relocate, but it still felt like Ammu had abandoned her.

He was her dad's younger brother, barely an adult yet when her mom died, but he'd swept in with his gangly limbs and goofy smile and made everything, if not better, bearable in time. Her father had been pretty useless in the days and weeks following. She remembers finding him weeping on the kitchen floor and crawling into his lap where he held her as they rocked together. That's pretty much all he did for a while. Instead, it was Aamir who made preparations for the funeral, who made sure she had food to eat and clothes to wear. Aamir, who soothed her back to sleep when she woke from dreams about that study door and the things behind it.

To be honest, Mariam is surprised this is the first time the others have woken up to her screaming. In the four days she's spent with them, she's slept better than she has in years, damp blankets and constant mosquito bites notwithstanding. Maybe it's Eun-Ji's reassuring snore or Camila's habit of mumbling in her sleep, but whatever it is, it's nice. Too bad it can't last.

On top of all that, the paranoia that she's being watched is back. Not what she needs right now.

Mariam leans against the tree she's attacked, slides to the ground, and starts to cry.

SOMEONE COMES CRASHING through the foliage. Mariam hears them coming a mile away and is able to compose herself accordingly. Nothing she can do about the gashes she's left in the tree above her head or the inevitable blotchiness of her face that just screams, "Hey! I've been crying!" but hey.

When the leaves part, there's Camila, a can in her hand with what looks to be food. Her eyes flicker between Mariam, her hatchet, and the tree she's been savaging, then she bumbles in Mariam's direction and thrusts the can at her.

"I, um. I thought you'd like some breakfast. Eun-Ji started clearing away the, well. Uh. Here, if you want."

Camila is blushing, and Mariam has the feeling this is going to turn into a conversation she does not want to have.

"Thaaaaanks," she drawls, taking the can and peering inside. Carrots and more tuna. Well, it's better than eating fruit again.

"So, uh, I." Camila's face turns a raspberry shade and the words tumble out of her mouth. "The first week I had a lot of nightmares about how my family died."

"Oh yeah?" Mariam thinks she sees exactly where this is going. She refuses to look up at Camila.

"Yeah. I mean, uh...there wasn't much left of my house. And I know it's probably not true, but what if, I mean, what if it's the whole West Coast? Most of my family, the ones I know anyways, they live here. Even if not everywhere is like this, what if enough of it is? And everyone is—what if they're all dead? And I don't know if I believe in last rites, but what if they're important?"

"Last rites?" Now Mariam does look up, curious despite herself.

"Yeah, y'know, like Catholic ones? My mom never really believed in that stuff, but my dad does—or he did. What if they're gone, and they couldn't get last rights? What if..." Camila takes a deep breath, blinking away the moisture in her eyes. "I have so many nightmares about that."

Mariam's annoyance melts away into something softer. She looks, really looks at Camila for the first time. Acid scars on her arms, the plaid piece of fabric around her right wrist, her left hand buried in her long hair, scratching the back of her head. She's young. She's scared.

They all are, Mariam included, and somehow they're all still here.

She sighs. Okay, maybe she owes Camila a bit of explanation.

"My mom committed suicide when I was a little older than Hana. I found her. Still get nightmares. That's all."

Camila sits beside her, the frenzied panic from her own grief melting away into pensiveness. Thank God it's not pity. Mariam doesn't think she could handle that, not right now.

"That sucks."

"It does," Mariam agrees.

"So, is this going to be a thing? The nightmares, I mean."

Mariam shrugs. "Probably. Maybe not? I'm not sure."

Camila nods, then motions to the tree and the sap-oozing gashes in its trunk. "This, uh. You okay?"

Mariam sighs and rolls her eyes. Why the hell she answers, she'll never know. Maybe she just needs someone to talk to. "I don't know. I'm used to it, you know? I've had these nightmares since I was really little, and...and..." Her voice cracks.

Mariam begins to cry. Again. Ugh.

Camila scoots closer and puts her good hand on Mariam's back, rubbing in soothing circles.

"Hey. It's all right. You don't have to talk about it if you don't want. I'm just, I mean, we were all kind of worried about you after this morning. Yeah, you have weird regenerative powers and that thing—" She looks at the hatchet, then back to Mariam. "—is seriously scary, but you're still, I don't know, it just seems like a lot."

Mariam laughs, her voice choked. "It is a lot." She swallows, closes her eyes, and leans her head against the tree. Goddamn, her head is so itchy!

"I can leave," Camila offers, starting to stand when Mariam's fingers ghost over her arm.

"Nah. Stay. I think I'm done moping. It'll be nice to just sit here for a while. Maybe talk? About, I don't know, stuff?" She manages a wobbly smile.

Mariam feels oddly exposed, but when Camila smiles and stays, it feels like maybe things are going to be okay.

IT'S HOT. HOTTER than hot, even though the sun is still, as always, just a suggestion of brightness behind the distant canopy. Mosquitoes buzz around their ankles as they walk in search of the hills, the edge of the forest, maybe even a decent camp: one with built-in shelter that won't let the night rains soak them to the bone. It's hard, though, because anywhere promising so far has been either unstable or already occupied. Ishmael and Mariam went together to check out a house that looked pretty sturdy, only to find a garland of human feet in various stages of decay adorning the doorframe. They didn't stay to find out who put them there, but Mariam suspects it was one of the fresh bodies they saw clustered around the back gate.

Those aren't the only bodies they encounter. Freshly dead corpses seem to manifest whenever Mariam strays away from camp, and it's beyond eerie. She stumbles upon them tangled into the ferns, leaning up against trees, and once hanging in a net of vines right at eye level. That was alarming.

They haven't found anything particularly gruesome today, but even so, the kids are getting tired. Hana has already given up on walking, instead riding up on Ishmael's shoulders, half asleep except for when she reaches up to scratch behind her ears, or Ishmael's. He likes that. They all do, in fact, and have been itching and scratching at their heads since the morning. Luci seems about going crazy with it, mussing her afro-textured curls with both hands as she stomps along behind Ishmael. Finally, Eun-Ji stops and turns to them, herself rubbing a hand over her scalp.

"We need to take a break. Get some water. Do something about" —she gestures to Luci, still itching— "this."

No one protests. Luci and Carlos flop down where they were standing, Carlos going into full sprawl so he can rub his head against the ground. Ishmael sits with a sigh and begins removing his prosthesis, massaging the limb with one hand and scratching his head with the other.

Mariam gives her own scalp a scratch, sighs, stretches, and then steps over to where Camila is struggling to take off her pack with only one hand and helps her out of the straps.

"Sit down, I'll get the water," she says, and Camila just nods. They're all so tired.

Eun-Ji and Mariam pass around the water bottles that they set up to catch the rain every night. Mariam suspects some kind of gross apocalypse juice is getting in there too, but there's nothing they can do about that, and there isn't exactly some of the fresh bottled stuff lying around for them to drink.

Once everyone has gulped down some of the warm greenish water, they sit in silence for a while, recovering their strength. Occasionally someone reaches up to scratch, but even that feels like too much effort. When Hana crawls into Eun-Ji's lap to fall asleep, Eun-Ji cards her fingers through the little girl's hair almost absentmindedly, but then she grimaces and pulls back.

"Oh no, I thought this might be the problem," she says, picking through Hana's hair more deliberately.

"What is it?" Ishmael asks, peering over to where Eun-Ji is sitting.

"We have lice."

Chapter Six

MARIAM IS BACK from her trip to the abandoned Target. No canned goods to be found, and the stench of rotting produce and meat just about made her gag, but the razors were still mostly there, along with some scissors, and she'd even found some lice shampoo. She threw it in the backpack just in case. She'd picked up clothes and some new blankets too, hopefully lice-free this time, wondering why the hell they didn't just go to Target to begin with instead of pilfering from abandoned houses. Even the Target stuff smells pretty musty, but no one complains.

When Hana realizes what's going to happen, she throws herself at her mother's feet, begging, "Eomma, Eomma, please don't cut my hair! Please, I don't want to look like a boy again! I'll be so good! I'll walk and not make Ishmael carry me, and I'll help with making food and I'll even put on my shoes! Eomma, please!"

Eun-Ji picks her up off the ground and soothes her daughter. "I'm so sorry, my love. This isn't a punishment, you have been good, but we need to get rid of these lice. I am so sorry. I am so sorry." Hana pushes her away and goes straight to Mariam, who is at a loss as to what this tantrum is about.

"You won't make me look like a boy, will you? You won't let them cut my hair. You're my friend!"

"It's just a little haircut, kiddo. No big deal, right?"

"No! Everyone said I was a boy before, but I'm not! My hair makes people see I'm a girl." Hana's lip trembles and tears threaten to spill over again.

Eun-Ji scoops Hana up again, and this time Hana puts her little face into Eun-Ji's shoulder and sobs. "She's trans, Mariam. The hair is a big deal to her."

Mariam understands, then, and tries to find words. When they do come, they're gentle. "Hana, I'm sorry. I don't want to cut your hair, but your mom is right. We have to get rid of the lice—all of us."

Hana calms down a bit once she understands everyone is getting their hair cut, not just her, and after Eun-Ji explains that lots of pretty ladies have short hair, but Hana still isn't too happy.

When the time to actually cut the hair comes, Mariam goes first. She sits between Eun-Ji's legs and almost sighs in relief as the blade slides over her head. She'll be much cooler this way, without her thick black hair to trap in the heat.

Eun-Ji is next, so she and Mariam trade positions.

"See?" Eun-Ji says when it's over, her long black hair lying in pieces around her. She cradles a sobbing and resigned Hana in her lap. "It's not so bad. I'm still your Eomma, and I still look like a girl."

Mariam hands a pair of scissors and a razor to Eun-Ji and is about to call for Carlos when Camila comes forward.

"You can do mine," she says to Mariam, and Hana cries harder.

"But how will I comb it if, if, if you—you cut it?" Hana wails, hiccups interrupting her words, reaching out to grab Camila's dark waves. Camila kneels before her and puts the child's sticky hand to her cheek.

"I know. And I love having long hair. But I have lice, too. We have to do this to stop the itching."

Then she sits before Mariam, and smiling, holds Hana's hand as they both settle into place. Eun-Ji runs her fingers through Hana's hair and presses a kiss to the top of her head before picking up the scissors, taking great care not to nick her scalp when the scissors are no longer useful.

THEY SLEEP MORE peacefully during the warm nights with their hair shorn and the lice gone. Even if Hana starts to sniffle every time she reaches up to play with the hair that is no longer there, at least the incessant itching has stopped. Their new clothes stink less, their blankets are cleaner, and eventually, they settle into a new routine.

It is a little odd to see Camila without her trademark long hair, Mariam thinks. Camila's hair had been something else, and while she doesn't look any less pretty without it, she does look different. But Mariam will get used to it. Just like she got used to not shaving or brushing her teeth or bathing. Oh God, does she miss bathing.

It's no small relief, then, when after days of hacking their way through the forest they hear the sound of rushing water. No one says anything for a while—it might be too much to hope for—but after not too long it becomes undeniable.

As the trees begin to thin out, Luci gives a whoop and runs toward the sound, shouting, "Hey, guys, look what I found! It's a river! A big one! And look, you can see the sky!"

Ishmael climbs up beside her and gives a low whistle. "Looks like the Los Angeles River is back," he says.

"I wanna see; I wanna see!" Hana runs up to them and clutches Luci's leg to keep her balance on the bank. "Whoa. That's cool."

Mariam and the others follow not far behind, and yeah, cool is right. Probably this is one of those places where the river was hemmed in by concrete, a narrow strip of dingy water that barely deserved the name. Now, though, it's a rushing expanse of current, tinted blue because, wow, you can see the sky, and it's glorious.

They stare a while, drinking in the sunshine and the way it bounces off the water. Carlos strips off his shirt and lies down on the mossy bank, his brown skin turning gold in the light.

After a few moments, it's Camila who suggests, "Maybe we should wash clothes and take baths?"

Mariam really, really likes the sound of that. Like, a lot. But, "Maybe not wash our clothes. They might never get dry again," she suggests.

Eun-Ji must have heard them because she fairly bounds up beside them in her haste. There's an uncharacteristic grin spreading across her face.

"Bathing?" she says, and glances between them with a spark in her dark eyes. "That's the best idea I've heard in weeks."

With Eun-Ji's permission, Mariam hikes a ways down the bank until she finds a place where the river widens and slows, where the current probably won't whisk them away or suck them down into its weedy belly as long as they're careful. The others join her, and in the end, it's decided they'll go in shifts: Ishmael and Carlos; Mariam, Camila, and Luci; and then Eun-Ji and Hana.

The water's cool despite the heat that shimmers over the surface, and no one minds in the least. It's a clean cold, not the clammy damp of nights in the forest, and a welcome escape from the cloying heat that sticks to their skin the rest of the time. They use the lice shampoo instead of soap because they don't have anything else, and it's really not that bad an idea so long as they avoid their more sensitive bits. Mariam wishes she'd grabbed some other hygiene products, and she vows that the next abandoned grocery store they find, she will definitely raid for proper soap. As it is, it's not bad.

When it's their turn, she, Camila, and Luci all turn away from each other and pass the bottle of shampoo between them. Mariam tries to grab the bottle out of the air when Camila throws it to her with a "Mariam, catch!" but it falls into the moving water and Mariam has to swim after it to keep it from getting lost. After all, Eun-Ji and Hana haven't had a chance to take baths yet.

When she comes back, it's with mischief in her heart, and she splashes at both Camila and Luci. Camila splutters, but Luci laughs and joins in, and soon they're all splashing and swimming and Mariam doesn't even notice she's staring at Camila until the blushing girl manages, "What?"

Mariam shakes her head, heat rising in her cheeks to match Camila's, before spluttering, "Nothing."

Luci interrupts the moment with a sound of annoyance and by dousing the both of them in water.

The river water feels refreshing in a way that rainwater doesn't, and it's so good to be clean, Mariam wants to shout for the sheer joy of it. When they're finished, they scramble dripping onto the bank and spend a moment or two lying in the sun. The light pulls the chill of the water out of their bones and gilds them in warmth.

Getting into their dirty, damp clothes after is less fun, but still. They needed this. Joy is a rare emotion to come by these days.

It's short-lived because not long after they've all dried off and gathered around a couple of cans of lima beans, Ishmael motions for Mariam and Camila to join him and Eun-Ji a little ways away from the kids.

He's shaking his head, and says quietly, "We have a problem. If this is the river, then there's no way we've been heading north. Northeast at best, but most likely we've been going east all this time. We're probably south of downtown by now. I must have gotten us turned around. I'm really sorry. It's so—" He pauses to make an exasperated sigh. "—dang difficult to figure out which way is which when you can't see the sky."

Mariam shakes her head and laughs, but it doesn't come out as bitter as she thought it would.

"Um, that bath was totally worth getting turned around. And anyways—" She sobers. "—I really didn't think we would be getting through the forest no matter where we went. It's, like I said, a wall. Even if the military is still trying to get in after who knows how long—"

"Seven weeks," Eun-Ji interrupts.

"After seven weeks, I doubt we'd be able to do anything. I saw them trying to get through with a chainsaw, and the vines just grew back. And like, we haven't seen any sign that anyone's looking for survivors. No planes, no helicopters, nothing. Don't you think we would have heard something by now? LA is usually crawling with helicopters. There are three major airports. There should have been something. So, I mean. I don't know. I don't think that's the smartest way to spend our energy anyways."

Mariam is bad at comfort. The hopelessness on their faces makes her wish she hadn't said anything but done is done. She doesn't really have enough optimism to go around.

"Let's just focus on surviving for now," she tries, but except for Eun-Ji, it doesn't seem to have the intended effect.

ON THE DAY they find the overpass, it's raining like Mariam has never, ever seen rain before. It started with a few warm drips on their faces as they lay asleep, and at first, she thinks it'll be the same as always, a thin mist drifting down through the trees to dampen but not drown them. But by the time they're awake and packing away the blankets, water bounces and dribbles off every surface, streaming down the trees and welling up out of the moss to fill their shoes.

They'd tried to cover their heads with towels, but that lasts all of a minute before those too are soaked through. They might as well have washed their clothes when they'd had the chance because it's going to be a long time before anything dries after this.

Despite the lingering heat, the rain brings cold with it too, and soon they're all shivering, so the only thing to do is move. Ishmael rallies the kids into a straggly little line and they set off to go find that shelter they've been hoping for. They keep the river close, only straying far enough into the trees to keep away from the unstable bank and the current that's gotten far less friendly with the onset of the downpour.

It's a miserable journey, and the rain is not even a little sympathetic. They must look a sight: bald, soggy, and trudging through water up to their ankles. Both Hana and Carlos have dissolved into tears, not that anyone can tell the difference between that and the water running down their faces. Everyone is exhausted, and the rain makes visibility nil.

That's why it's such a surprise when a dark gash in the trees opens up in front of them. Mariam wants to urge caution, but Luci is already running forward, splashing over the sodden dirt onto the higher ground inside the cave. Cave, because that's what it looks like, though Mariam can't fathom why there would be a cave in the jungle, in the middle of what used to be a city. Still, she is in no mood to be picky, and they're all wet and cold enough that a respite from the leaking sky feels like it might be worth confronting whatever is lurking in the dark.

"Oh my God," Luci enthuses as she begins wringing out her shirt. "I thought I'd never be dry again."

"You're technically not," Ishmael says with a snort. "We're all soaked through."

Mariam barely registers their exchange. She puts her hand against one of the walls, surprised to find dry concrete under her fingertips. The ceiling, what she can see of it in the dim light, is a smooth slope that disappears into the blackness at the far end of the cave. Aside from the soft voices of the others, she can't hear anything. It seems safe enough, for now.

"We need a fire," Ishmael says after teasing Luci some more, and he's right, they're all freezing. The question is, where are they going to find something dry enough to burn when the entire world is pretty much swimming? It's already hard enough when the forest is at its usual level of uncomfortable damp.

Sometimes it seems like they can never catch a break, but right now is not one of those times. Just as Mariam is resigning herself to venturing back out in the rain in search of wood, Eun-Ji emerges from another corner of the cave, still soaked but beaming, with an armful of branches and twigs.

"There's a tree under here!" she says, a little breathless with the excitement of her find, "All smashed to pieces, but dry! It must be from before."

It still takes a while to get the fire going, but after it's done, they strip down to their underthings, Ishmael removes his prosthesis with a sigh of relief, and they all huddle close to warm themselves.

In the flickering light, it becomes apparent the cave is the collapsed remnant of an overpass, all overgrown on the outside but dry and mostly moss-free on the inside. At the far end, where the ceiling meets the asphalt of the floor, there's a mess of broken concrete and a twisted hunk of rusty metal that was probably a car, once. The tree Eun-Ji found is there too, and it's good to see, somehow, with its papery leaves that look nothing like the giant, spongy things that dominate everywhere else. It's a relic of the old normal, and oddly comforting.

The rain makes a shimmery curtain at the mouth of the cave, and it's impossible to see anything in the dark out there. Inside, though, the fire lights their faces, tired but content. In the morning, when the sky is lighter and hopefully composed of more air than liquid, they can decide on whether or not they want to stay, but for now, at least, it feels a bit like it could be home.

Dinner is chicken soup warmed up in the can over the fire, and afterward, they sit back with their bellies full of the hot broth, the glow of the fire on their skin. Hana and

Carlos are arguing, as usual, but there's no malice in it, just two bickering kids who've forgotten, for the moment, that the world outside their cave has been shaken to bits and eaten alive. Eun-Ji and Ishmael watch them, laughing along whenever Carlos says something outrageous, Eun-Ji with her head leaning on Ishmael's broad shoulder.

Luci seems to be doing a bit better, too. It's been a while coming, but she's not as depressed as she'd been, and right now, she's organizing some of their things to dry in the warmth of the cave. When she's done, she sits between Carlos and Hana and starts to teach them a clapping game that Mariam recognizes from her childhood.

Camila scoots over to sit next to Mariam and just watches the fire for a moment.

"Hey, how's your wrist?" Mariam asks after a moment, giving Camila's arm a little tap just above the elbow.

"Um, it's a bit sore, but not, you know, nearly as painful as it was. It's getting better."

"It still hurts?"

"Not much. It just kinda aches, you know?"

Mariam nods. "If you let me, I might be able to help with that. Just a little bit, nothing, like, too helpful."

Camila smiles. "Sure. How?"

Mariam holds out her hands. "Give me your wrist?"

"Okay."

Mariam rubs the muscles above Camila's wrist, working her way up her arm. The tension in Camila's face drops, and her eyes begin to close. After a few minutes, Mariam stops, and Camila looks at her hazy-eyed.

"Where'd you learn that? It felt really nice. My wrist feels a lot less painful. Very nice."

"My uncle taught me," Mariam says, and there's a little twinge in her chest. "He was a massage therapist."

"You're really good." Camila scoots closer.

"He was better."

Camila rolls her eyes and leans against Mariam. "I'm so sleepy now. I'm totally relaxed."

Mariam laughs, grateful Camila isn't pushing about Uncle Aamir.

Camila leans back against the wall of the cave to watch the kids, and, man, she's awfully pretty with the firelight on her cheeks and her mouth creased in a smile. Mariam's chest twinges again, but this time it prompts her to reach out, covering Camila's fingers with her own.

Camila looks down, smiles, and interlaces her fingers with Mariam's.

MORNING ARRIVES LOUD and green, and they stumble out of the overpass to see what kind of spot they've found. It's a clearing, of sorts. Huge trees, thicker even than some of the redwoods Mariam's visited, make a ring around the cave's entrance, and the vines growing between their branches nearly block out the sky, but there's space enough for a fire and for them all to crowd around it if they wanted to. It's near the river, too, maybe 100 yards off.

They spend the morning cleaning up the cave and making camp. Eun-Ji sets out some of their things to dry, while Ishmael makes a loop of the area to make sure it's safe.

There are things to be scavenged from the surrounding area, and a little convenience store that Ishmael had noticed during the rainstorm to be explored.

How he noticed amidst all the gloom and the driving sheets of water is beyond Mariam, but he has sharp eyes and it doesn't really surprise her. She offers to go check it out, and, to get the bouncing four-year-old out of Eun-Ji's hands, takes Hana with her.

Maybe a mistake. Not even five minutes in, Hana whines, "Mariaaaaaaam. I'm tiiiiired." Mariam turns to find the little girl on the ground in a pouting heap, looking up at her with her eyes big and her lip stuck out and—of course—her arms held out to be carried.

Mariam sighs. Hana had positively begged to be allowed to come along with her to forage for supplies, and when they'd set off from camp, she'd been her usual buzzing self, all giggles and not even a whiff of complaint in the air.

But she's four years old, and Mariam's got strength in her legs for both of them.

"Up you come, baby," she says, and reaches down to scoop Hana off the ground.

With Hana settled on her back, Mariam sets off again, extra careful now that she's top-heavy, laden with a Hana whose knees dig uncomfortably into her sides.

Mariam doesn't mind, though, because today's been a good day: no rain, no bug bites—yet, and there's even the hint of a breeze slipping between the trees. She can deal with an overly affectionate kid clinging to her neck.

Hana really must have been tired, because she doesn't bounce or kick her feet, and after a while, even her quiet humming drops off into silence. The only sounds are the squish and crackle of Mariam's shoes on the forest floor and those far-off clicks and whistles that remind them that this forest is more alive than it should be.

She thinks Hana's fallen asleep, but after a while, she stirs, nuzzles her face into the back of Mariam's head, and says, "You smell nice."

Mariam is flattered, really, because Hana is too little to know how to lie about things like that.

"Thanks, Han—"

"—but Eomma smells nicer."

Ha. Okay, she'll grant her that. Eun-Ji probably does smell nice. Mariam gives Hana's legs a squeeze.

"You really love your mama, huh?"

"Yeah," Hana says and they lapse back into silence for a while. Mariam suspects Hana's dozing again until there's a voice, quiet, at her ear.

"Mariam, where's your Eomma?"

She hadn't been expecting that, and the surprise of it sends Mariam stumbling until she almost spills them both onto the moss. She catches herself with one hand on a tree, the other still supporting Hana. Her Eomma? Her mama is dead dead dead like everyone else, everyone, and she's going to cry—

She laughs in what she hopes is a casual way instead, and starts walking again, says, "I'm too old for a mama, Hana."

"No, you're not."

"Yes, I—" She stops, because, really, there's no arguing with Hana and she's right, besides. "Okay, I'm not too old for a mama. But mine is...she's far away."

"Far away..." Hana says slowly. "...that's what Carlos says about his Eomma."

Mariam considers. "What does Carlos mean by that?"

"Carlos's Eomma died. He told me." Here Hana pauses, and her little fingers tap gently at Mariam's collarbone. "Is that what you mean too?"

There's a lump in Mariam's throat, now, and a little wobble in her ankles. The breeze has picked up, miraculously, ruffling the vegetation around them until the forest is whispering.

The sound cocoons them in, and Mariam says, "Yeah. Like Carlos," and then, louder, to carry over the wind and the waving leaves, "My mom is far away like Carlos's."

Hana says nothing, but a moment later her arms are tightening around Mariam's neck in a hug, and her mouth makes a gentle pucker behind Mariam's ear.

"You can share my Éomma if you want. Carlos does."

"Yeah? Thanks, kiddo. Your mom's pretty great."

They reach the store they'd been looking for not long after, just a mound of moss and tangles that's slightly more upright than the other mounds of moss and tangles that surround it. Frankly, Mariam's surprised they've managed to find it at all, given the state of the place. How did Ishmael manage to see it through the pouring rain?

Mariam shakes the question away and sets Hana down outside, telling her to wait while she pokes her head in the crooked door. There's no movement, and it looks safe, so she takes Hana's hand and they step into the green-tinted gloom inside.

It's one of those little convenience stores with lighters (useful), snacks (all spoiled), beer (bottles shattered and cracked), and a rack of keychains that Hana finds irresistible. She lets go of Mariam's hand and plops herself down on the floor (this slimed with an oozy, greyish fungus—they'll have to wash clothes later) in front of the display. Then she turns, wide-eyed, to Mariam, and points to the keychains. It's a question, clearly.

Mariam smiles. "You can take whatever you want, you know. Nobody owns this stuff anymore."

"Really?"

"Really. Have a ball. I'll be over here, okay?"

Hana doesn't answer because she's already picking out her favorites. As Mariam browses the shelves for salvageable items, she keeps an eye on the little girl in the shop's security mirror. She watches as Hana takes down the colorful trinkets one by one and clips them to her ears, her sleeves, the hem of her dress. They jingle every time she moves.

When Mariam's pack is full of toothpaste, Band-Aids, and lighters, she comes back to the front. Hana's still crouched in front of the display.

"Ready to go?" Mariam asks.

Hana stands, less jingly now, but with her hands full of keychains.

"I got these," she says. "There's one for you, one for Camila, one for Eomma, one for Ishmael, Luci, and Carlos."

Mariam's mouth crooks in a smirk and she nods towards Hana's dress, still adorned with her first picks. "And six for you, I see."

"Yes. Six for me!" Hana grins up at her like she knows she's the cutest little button in the rainforest. Then she goes serious. "You should get one for your Eomma too."

"You think so?"

"She would like it."

Mariam hesitates, but then, "I think she would. What do you recommend?"

Hana turns and examines the display, a little less full now, and runs her fingers over the remaining keychains until she stops and plucks one off the rack.

"This one." She holds it out towards Mariam, a little black music note on a silver chain. "Because you like to sing. Does your Eomma like to sing?"

"Yeah, yeah she did. Thanks, Hana." Mariam takes the keychain and rubs it between her thumb and forefinger a moment before slipping it into her pocket. Somehow, it does feel like a gift for her mom. Something to carry until the time is right.

"Let's head home, okay? You'll have to walk all the way. My pack's too heavy now."

"I can do it!" Hana exclaims and bounces toward the door, still jingling and with her pockets full of presents.

Mariam hefts her bag on her shoulder and follows. "Yeah, I know you can. Wait for me, kid."

Back at the cave, the others accept their keychains with bemusement for the most part, indulging Hana as she prances around bestowing her gifts with an exaggerated magnanimity and poorly suppressed excitement. Her favorites get clipped onto her dress, tinkling like bells every time she moves, at least until Eun-Ji declares that it's time to do laundry. Then the keychains come off, and so does the dress. Hana pouts for all of ten minutes before she gets distracted by a lizard.

As she undresses, Mariam takes the music note out of her pocket and stashes it carefully in the folds of her bedding, taking a moment to run her thumb up and down its edges before she puts it away.

Chapter Seven

THAT EVENING, CAMILA'S steady breathing sends Mariam easy into a contented slumber, but sometime in the night, her dreams turn loud and twisted, full of voices and crawling skin. In the dark of the cave, she tosses fretfully.

"You'll never hurt again. Do you understand, sweetie? No more scraped knees, no more pain. All you have to do is shake his hand."

She's breathing in heaving gasps, tears running down her scrunched-up face as she breathes too fast. Her head feels dizzy, and the moon's light is too bright.

"Da-daddy, I do-don't want to!"

"Be a good girl and shake his hand. For me, Mariam." He's getting impatient now.

"But—"

"Damnit!" He sinks to his knees and shakes her tiny shoulders. "Do you want to end up like your mother? Please! Please just shake his hand. If I could do it for you I would, but Mariam, I can't." He's angry but crying too, tears of desperation and fear.

In the corner stands that monster, with its peeling skin and terrible voice. Its fraying robes brush the stain on the carpet.

"Come, child." It motions her close with a skeletal hand. Her father pushes her forward roughly, and she's too startled by her father's violence to do anything but obey. She reaches out with trembling fingers. She doesn't want to touch this thing! But Daddy's crying and Mommy is...no, she doesn't want to be put in the ground and buried under all that dirt like Mommy. She doesn't want her brains in her hair and blood leaking out her head.

She wants to live.

Their hands meet, and a light engulfs Mariam, humidity sinking into her every pore. She cries out, her voice a tiny squeak in the face of what sounds like a hundred horrifying voices laughing. Heat engulfs her hand where the Monster's fingers are wrapped around hers, but then her skin knits together, the brand invisible.

Her father is sobbing with relief and grabs her from the monster's clutches. Her hand feels slimy, and she buries her face in her father's shoulder.

"There," he chokes. "It's done. Nothing can ever hurt you again."

MARIAM WAKES WITH a start from the memory-turned-dream and finds her head resting on Camila's sharp shoulder. Camila stirs, mumbling something about wanting to be the blue lobster, and Mariam smiles despite the churning in her stomach. Dream logic is weird, but she's glad Camila's subconscious seems to be kinder than her own.

Because the dream has unsettled her. It was too real—too exact a memory of an event she hasn't thought of in years. Details she thought she'd forgotten. *Nothing can ever hurt you again*, he'd said. Well, that turned out to be a lie, but then, what else did they expect from a deal with the devil?

It's quiet outside, except for the occasional hoot or screech, but Mariam doubts she'll be getting back to sleep anytime soon. She's sitting up, staring at the dying embers of their fire when the hairs on the back of her neck rise.

That feeling of being watched is back again, and when she hears something moving in the darkness, she bolts up and heads toward it, all but ignoring the fact that she's not wearing anything but her underwear. A startled Camila makes some confused noises, but Mariam ignores her in favor of grabbing her shirt where it's drying by the fire and following a rustling slither through the undergrowth. Maybe it's just a harmless little garden snake, but she has a weird feeling it's not: something strange is going on. And besides, even if it is just a snake, in this strange new world, that could be a threat too. She pulls the shirt over her torso and runs after the slithering thing.

The glow of the cave has almost disappeared into the darkness behind her, and she's about to give up on her pursuit when it's cut short. She slams into something solid and warm, and oh, it's just Dad.

Wait, Dad?

Then it hits her.

She lets out a string of curses, then manages to demand, "What the hell are you doing here, Daddy? Where on earth have you been?" Heat blooms in her face, and she wishes she had the hatchet. It wouldn't hurt him, it couldn't hurt him, but it would make her feel better.

"Such language, Mariam." Her father frowns at her, then straightens, cracks his neck. There's something weird about him, or weirder than usual, and it sends unease down her spine to coil in her gut and mingle with the anger there.

"I'm looking out for my little girl, is all. How've you been?" he asks conversationally, leaning against a tree.

Mariam's jaw clenches once, twice, and then she splutters, "How've I...how've I been? Daddy. Take a look around you. How do you think I've been?"

He shrugs, and even in the dark, she can see the way his shoulders crook up too high and come down again with an unnatural snap.

"Well. You're alive, aren't you?"

Something about that stings. He'd always been so concerned with her safety. What's happened to him? Mariam tamps her anger down a notch to get a good look at her father. He's the same—or almost the same. Same pressed suit, somehow wrinkle-free and pristine even in this soggy hell-scape. Same hair, slick and smooth over his head. It's his face, she decides, his face which is twitching in and out of shape, like there's something else, another face maybe, trying to escape from under his skin. Mariam swallows hard.

"Um. Are you all right? I couldn't find you. I didn't know where you..." She trails off and hesitates before reaching up to touch his shoulder.

He recoils slightly, tenses, then relaxes into a cavalier smile. Her hand falls back to her side.

"Right as rain, sweetie. I'm here now, just popping in to see how you're doing. Kind of...avoiding someone right now, but that's to be expected."

"Oh, God. Please tell me you didn't piss off that *Thing* again."

Her father motions around him, chuckling, almost giggling: the laughter of a child who can't believe his luck. "Well. If this whole carnivorous rainforest situation is any indication, I'd say maybe I have?"

Understanding comes slowly, because what could that possibly mean? But when it does, it comes all at once.

Mariam's heart sinks then leaps, her anger rekindled and hotter than ever. "Do you mean to tell me," she says with trembling calm, "that all this is your fault?"

He smiles, and, oh, it's a smile. There are teeth in that smile. "Perhaps."

Now, her voice comes out low, dangerous. "Do you know how many people have died? How many people are still dying?" She thinks of Hana then, and her shorn head, of Luci's pain at having lost her baby sister, and her new family's daily struggle just to stay alive in this place. "How many good and decent people are suffering because you are never satisfied with what you've got? Always another spell, another deal. You could never leave well enough alone. Well, now look! What was this even supposed to achieve, Dad? All of this, and for what?"

He taps her nose like he used to when she was a child. "Ah, but that's where you're wrong. See, I've figured it out. I have everything now. Power. Security. Eternal life."

Mariam's blood slows in her veins and she feels like she's been slapped across the face. "What?"

"Well, I found a loophole. You remember how it was. All that time in the study, all those late nights and missed holidays, you know I was looking for one thing: a way to protect us from ending up like your mother, a way for us two to live forever. The Beast offered me a way in: if I took Its place as ruler of the dead, I would never die. And I could save you, too.

"It said it was the only way. But what It didn't count on is that I'm a lawyer, honey. Your father's a damn good lawyer, and that Beast can hardly read!" He pauses to contain the grin that's stretching his cheeks beyond their natural limits. "I've been trying to find a way to get around that clause for years, and a couple of months ago it dawned on me: yes, I'll have to take Its place. But you see, It never did say when. So I put it in the contract, just the way I wanted it, and now I'm free to wander until I get bored and decide to go sit in the underworld forever. Eternal. Life."

"So you made the deal. You made the deal to live forever where you become the devil." It's not a question. Mariam is stunned, but she understands perfectly well. Oh, God. But then, she doubts even God could save her father now.

"Essentially," he says, seemingly unaware of how close Mariam is to breaking his face, or trying to, for all the good it would do. "It's just unhappy I found a way to avoid the whole thing indefinitely. Eventually, I'll have to take over, but not before I've had my fun. Could be years. Centuries, even. And you know, I can do it for you too! You and me, father and daughter, roaming the earth like gods. You've already taken the first step, remember? I tried to remind you. What do you say?"

"Daddy, what have you done?" Horror dawns anew in her chest and she backs away. Had he been in her head? Her dream—if she could really call it hers—is coming back to her again. She cradles her right hand to her chest, curling the fingers that still remember how the Beast held her hand and burned it without leaving a scar.

"Nothing I wouldn't do for my baby girl, Mariam. You know that," he says, and for a moment they're thinking of the same room, the same night and its everlasting consequences. Then her dad frowns and snaps to attention, his back too rigid to belong to a human, but she supposes he isn't really, not anymore. "Looks like we've got company. Your little girlfriend is cute, but I don't think it's quite time for her to meet me yet. Also, please put some trousers on next time." Malik smiles eerily once more before waving his fingers and shrinking down into a...snake? Well, that explains the slithering, but what is going on with her dad?

But then his words sink in and Mariam twirls to find Camila standing between the trees in nothing but her underwear.

"Um." Camila looks down at her bare toes in the mud.

"How long have you been there?"

"Hah, well, uh."

"Camila," Mariam demands, striding over to the shorter girl. "What did you hear?"

"I..." The words don't come for a moment, but then they do, in a tumbling stream. "Mariam, what do you mean this whole thing is your dad's fault? What did he mean by saying he could make you live forever?" She opens her mouth for another question, but her face turns white. She manages, "Does this mean...this whole thing could have been avoided?"

Mariam steps close. She's never used her height as an advantage before, but she does now, leaning over Camila so that she can growl into her face, "You shouldn't have been eavesdropping!"

To Camila's credit, she doesn't back down. "What the hell, Mariam? You were going off into the dark on your own. Was I supposed to let you? What if you'd gotten hurt?"

"Um, earth to Camila? I can't get hurt, remember?"

Camila gapes like a fish, then rubs her hands over her arms. "Well. I forgot." A light goes on behind her eyes. "Wait. Does the whole regeneration thing have something to do with...all of this?" She looks up at Mariam with fear and confusion.

Mariam sighs, and the anger is gone, replaced with guilt. "It's a long story."

"I've got time." Her voice is soft and hard all at once.

"Okay." Mariam supposes there's no hiding this anymore. "Fine. But, let's put something warm on, first."

THEY SIT BY the river and for the first time in forever, look up at the night sky. Without the light pollution, the sky is ablaze with starlight, and they drink in the view for a moment before Camila prompts, "No offense, but there's something seriously off about your dad."

Mariam sighs. "In case you haven't noticed, there's something seriously off about me, too"

"Yeah, but, you're not creepy. He is."

"He's complicated," Mariam shrugs. "After Mom died...she had cancer. She'd been in remission, but it was the third time, and she didn't want the radiation therapy or the chemotherapy and her odds just weren't good, so she ended it. That's what her letter said, anyways. And Dad, he was so worried about me, I guess, so he summoned this... this Thing that rules hell or something. The devil, I guess, but not really. And he made a deal with It, and now I can't get hurt. I can't get sick, and I can't die." Mariam laughs cynically then. "Trust me, I've tried it. It hurts like hell, but I can't die."

She's never admitted she's tried to hurt herself in that way before. When Dad had wrapped himself up in his black magic garbage for weeks on end and Ammu left for Baltimore, things got hard. Sure, she had her friends, but few of them understood parental death, and she wasn't sure how to broach the magic stuff. She was so lonely, and she was confused: about her mom, about Ammu going away, about normal teenage stuff, like how she couldn't decide if she wanted to go to the formal with Hunter or Pamela. So, she jumped off her dad's office building. That should have done it. She should have died. Instead, her bones snapped back together like Lego blocks and she took the bus home.

Camila seems not to have noticed her massive confession.

"You said you didn't know how you could regenerate."

"Well, I lied."

"Why?"

"Camila, seriously? Would you have believed me if I had told you my dad made a deal with the devil so I would have weird powers? Can you imagine?" She pitches her voice higher, brighter, in mocking tones. "'Oh, yeah, Daddy summoned the devil into our study so I couldn't ever die!' Do you honestly believe that would've gone over well?"

"I don't know!" Camila exclaims, apparently keeping herself from looking at Mariam's face. When she finally does turn to her, it's with accusation in her eyes. It hurts. A lot. "And this? The crazy animals and creepy plants and everyone being dead? Do you know how many people are dead, Mariam? Everyone—my friends, my family, my baby sister, my—Do you even know?"

Of course, she knows. But Mariam doesn't know what to say, so she just settles with, "Looks like Daddy bit off more than he could chew this time."

"Wow, that isn't cryptic." Camila practically spits, her big brown eyes narrowing into tiny slits.

Mariam's heart aches. "I don't know! He did something the Beast didn't like and now everyone is dead. Camila, I didn't know," she says, pleading. "I swear I didn't know. I only knew he was always trying to become more powerful. I didn't know that thing would try and kill everyone just because my dad is obsessed with living forever." The truth is, Mariam knows her dad did all this for her. She didn't ask for it, but her father did it anyway. All of this violence, all of this *death* that she can smell, on her clothes, in her hair, in the reek of the vines at her feet: it's her fault.

But she can't lose Camila and she can't lose the others.

"How do I know you're not lying again?" Camila's voice is wavering. "How do I know you're not involved?" She starts crying. "What if you're the reason that everyone—they're all gone?"

Mariam considers rubbing her back, and her hand is halfway there before she decides against it.

"Camila. What do I have to hide at this point? You saw everything. You know everything. My dad is next in line to be the—" Here she curses. "—devil, he's barely human anymore, and he wants to do it to me next. You think I want this? I lost people too, and watching you all struggle through this is...is...."

"Yeah, watching us struggle is hard, isn't it?" It bites, the bitterness, but then Camila softens. "How can I trust you?" There's hopelessness there, and it's breaking Mariam's heart.

"Camila. Please. There's nothing I haven't done for you guys." Mariam feels like maybe she's on the verge of tears, too. "Please trust me. Please. I think..." And here she goes, baring her heart for Camila to take or break, "I think I'd be miserable if you didn't."

Camila gets up and looks down at her, tears still shining in the moonlight. "Well, be miserable, then."

THEY DON'T TALK to each other the next day. Well, Mariam tries, but Camila avoids her. Carlos glowers at Mariam in solidarity, even though he's got no idea why Camila's mad. She knows Camila is Carlos's favorite person, and that's probably what this it.

Mariam takes some consolation in the fact that Camila hasn't told Eun-Ji and Ishmael what she knows. She's not sure they would forgive her, and she's not sure she would deserve it if they did.

But they don't know, at least not yet.

No one knows what to make of the sudden hostility between her and Camila, but there are more pressing things to worry about, like getting the blankets to dry and gathering food and making sure the little ones don't fall into the river as they crowd excitedly around its swollen banks, looking for tiny green frogs.

Mariam disappears for a while. She isn't sure she's coming back. Yeah, it'd suck to leave all her stuff behind, but she doesn't think she can stand Camila's ire. Much as she doesn't like to admit it, but that crush she didn't want? Well, maybe it happened, and maybe it was more than just a crush, and maybe she'd thought it was going somewhere. It hurts, it really really hurts that now it's all gone to hell. And the actual implications of what her father's done? She doesn't even want to begin processing that tangle of crap.

Mariam isn't really sure where she's headed when she stumbles upon a clearing filled with yellow flowers. Flowers. Camila likes flowers. Hana loves them. This could be something.

Mariam gets an idea. Flowers are good for one of two things: flower crowns and summoning the devil. She's seen it happen often enough. Don't ask her why, but plants seem to do the trick, whether it's fruit or flowers or even just fresh clippings. Forget blood sacrifices, the devil wants plants—seems to draw Its power from them.

And now the devil wants her dad, which, you know, sucks for him, but maybe if she could reason with It...the thought makes her sick, but what else is there for her to do? It's not fair to expect everyone to suffer for her dad's mistakes. Maybe turning him in is the best thing to do.

She hurriedly makes some flower crowns to take back to the others but saves the best ones for her sacrifice. She arranges them in a pattern she's seen her father make plenty of times, then glances around and pats her pockets. Plant life and something valuable, that's what her father always said. He always used money or her mom's jewelry or wine when he had the good stuff, but what does she have? Her fingers brush against something cool and smooth in her pocket: Hana's keychain. She pulls it out and rubs the little music note between her fingers for a moment. It'll have to do, and it's valuable enough, in its own way. Hopefully, the Beast agrees. She sets it down among the flowers, then sits back, takes a breath, and starts chanting the rhyme her father taught her on her eighth birthday. The words feel foreign in her mouth, but she plows on, even as she stutters through one or two phrases.

Nothing. The flowers don't wilt; there's no portal; nothing happens.

She tries again. This time, she makes sure she doesn't stumble on her words, but again, nothing. She feels tears sting at her eyes. Is it the keychain? The chant?

Mariam tries one more time, but her heart isn't in it, and when she fails again, she grabs the keychain. It must be just her imagination, but the metal seems hot to her touch, and she swears she feels something is watching her again, but the flowers are fine, and that Thing isn't here.

She leaves the clearing with her flower crowns and trudges back to the overpass, oblivious to the two pairs of eyes watching her from the trees.

Second Interlude

MALIK IS FUMING. He doesn't curse, but for the first time in his life, he's tempted to shout profanities at his daughter. What is she thinking? Is she out of her mind? That Thing would eat her alive if It could.

The only reason the Beast didn't come is because It didn't want to, and Mariam should thank her lucky stars that It didn't. Though if he's perfectly honest, he doesn't know why it didn't work. She did it correctly, and sentimental items are always more likely to bring the Beast than even the most expensive of wines. He'd watched her with the little girl on their trip to that convenience store. That keychain had "sentimental" written all over it.

Malik had stumbled upon the incantation—the whole idea really—after an eccentric client had given him the book. Some joke about attorneys being in bed with the devil—it didn't make sense even at the time. Malik had kept it though, letting it lurk on the corner of his study desk for months without even cracking the cover. Then Alexandra died, and he'd had a lot of time to sit and brood in that office. The book was just a distraction, at first.

Over time, it became everything.

He'd never thought it would get this far, and maybe if he still had much of a conscience it would bother him. As it is, he can hardly remember how he got here. Everything is confused these days, all the memories bleeding together in his head. Only a few things matter now: Mariam and the Beast that wants them both.

Surely the Beast knows where they are after Mariam's little trick, and Malik suspects that if things were a little different—if he hadn't said just the words he'd said and spilled the wine just so—that It would reach out and take them. Crush them. But there are rules, now. Agreements they've made.

Mariam is going to get them both in trouble, though, and while he can protect her and her friends from people, he can't do anything about the forest. Or the Beast.

Chapter Eight

SHE GOES OVER it in her mind again and again and can't figure out what she did wrong. Sentimental always beats monetary value, at least that's what Dad's always said. Maybe it was the incantation? But as awkward as the words felt, she's sure she got them right. She feels angry and sick, angry because it didn't work and sick because she was ready to trade her dad's life in for the lives of people she barely knows. Then again, seems like she barely knows her dad anymore too. A shiver runs through her spine as she recalls the way his face twitched and quivered, the way his shoulders hitched with an unnatural energy. Something has to be done.

As Mariam approaches camp with the flower crowns draped over her arm, she dispels the thoughts of betraying her dad and is met with a scene that puts the warmth back into her cold limbs.

The others are spread out around the entrance to their cave. Hana and Carlos are shuffling around on their hands and knees, busy trying to recapture the frogs they've brought from the river and subsequently allowed to escape. It's an admirable effort, but, as Luci drawls from her perch on a nearby log, "Give it up; you're never gonna catch them."

Hana notices Mariam's reappearance first, and crawls over to beam up at her and asks, "Are those flowers for me?"

Despite everything, Mariam breaks into a smile, because, really, there's not a soul alive who could say no to that face, and bends down to place the smallest crown on top of Hana's little head.

"Of course, baby," she says.

The way Hana lights up bright like a flower herself almost makes Mariam forget that she made these to right a wrong. Hana stands slowly, eyes rolled up to try and see the yellow petals on her forehead, and fingers fluttering at the crown where it brushes the tips of her ears. Her mouth opens wide in a smile and she's just perfect, a picture of delight in a blue dress.

Then Hana runs to Eun-Ji, crying, "Eomma, Eomma, look at me! Am I pretty? Do you think I'm pretty?"

And Eun-Ji laughs and catches her up in her arms. "You are always beautiful, darling, but these flowers do make you especially lovely."

"I have one for you too, Eun-Ji," Mariam says, shy for some reason, and extends one of the crowns toward her.

Eun-Ji takes it with a sincere smile and a "thank you," and then Ishmael is there at her shoulder, grinning from ear to ear and asking, "What about me?"

Mariam laughs, she can't help herself, and reaches up to drape one of the crowns over Ishmael's head. Hana plants a wet kiss on his cheek and fairly squeals with joy. Soon, everyone's got a halo of yellow petals around their ears, even Carlos, who at first turned his nose up at the offer but relented after only a few moments of squirming. Mariam, too, after Luci pointed out she wasn't wearing one yet.

Everyone except Camila, who hasn't moved from her seat in the mouth of the cave. She's very deliberately looking out toward the river, hands folded in her lap and mouth pursed. Mariam walks toward her with the last crown still looped in the crook of her elbow.

"Hey," she says, and it comes out croaky and quiet. She clears her throat and starts again. "Hey, do you want a flower crown?"

Camila turns, and Mariam can see the hard set of her jaw, the sharp line of her brow. The flowers are pretty, though, and Camila likes pretty things, she's learned. So she can see the battle, too, behind Camila's eyes, between her fingers twitching for the crown and the anger in the crease of her cheek.

She knows Camila sees this for what it is: a peace offering. The fact that she doesn't want to take it makes Mariam's heart drop into her belly. She opens her mouth to say something, then decides nah, she'd better not. There are far too many listening ears, and this isn't really a conversation Mariam wants to have with everyone around. Having Camila mad at her is hard enough. She doesn't think she can take it from anyone else.

It's Hana, of course, who saves Mariam from tears, when she skips over to pull the crown gently from Mariam's arm and places it on Camila's head, saying, "Now you're a princess, too!"

THE KIDS PRANCE around for a while with their hair full of flowers, but eventually they settle down, frogs and flowers equally forgotten. Camila hasn't moved. Mariam watches her from her seat near the fire, absentmindedly peeling a spiky fruit with her knife.

Morning slowly becomes afternoon, though it's hard to tell even in the relative bright of their clearing. It's clear and sunny near the riverbank. The kids wander over to laze on the shore, all stripped down to their underwear because really, no one cares at this point, and the sun just feels so nice after weeks and weeks trapped under the dense canopy.

They don't talk about it, but they seem to have come to the silent agreement that the overpass-turned-cave is their new home until they find something better or less exposed. No one has brought up plans for escaping the forest since that day by the river. This unspoken agreement is that this is it, for now. And it's not bad here. It's nice, really: cool during the day and warm when they need it to be courtesy of their little fire. It would be perfect—if only Camila were at least looking in her direction.

For now, though, there's still plenty to do around camp. Carlos has spotted a tree with fruits that look suspiciously like oranges hanging over the edge of the river not too far away from the cave, and Eun-Ji suggests that they go try to harvest some as a treat. Spiky passion-fruit-apples and old cans of soup are great, but an orange? An honest to goodness, real-life pre-apocalypse fruit? Now that would be something.

The tree turns out to be a little bit bigger than Carlos remembers, with long, moss-draped branches that swoop out over the river. Bunches of round, crimson fruits hang down almost far enough to touch the water. Okay, so maybe Carlos doesn't have a solid grasp on what oranges are supposed to look like, but the fruits do look good, and there's not a single thorn on them.

"Do you think we could reach them?" Luci asks, hopeful.

Eun-Ji hesitates. "Maybe, but the current...it might be too dangerous." She's right. The river is narrower here, and the water beneath the tree is pulling along at an alarming pace. One slip and you'd be half a mile downstream before you knew it.

Mariam looks around at the others and sees the quiet disappointment in their eyes. She volunteers to do the climbing.

It's a testament to how much they want this that no one protests much, even though it's probably a stupid risk to take for some fruit that like as not will end up being poisonous or filled with blind worms or not even fruit at all. Stuff like that happens, now. But in the end, Mariam ends up shimmying up into the tree and hanging upside-down from the nearly horizontal branches in order to pluck the fruits one by one and stash them in a makeshift sling they've fashioned out of a blanket. When it's almost full and her fingers are sticky with purplish juice that smells wonderful, she scoots back toward the shore, careful not to let the pendulous sling spill. The last part is a little tricky, though, with the heavy sack of fruit weighing her down enough to make the distance between her and the bank seem daunting.

Mariam considers and then looks to Camila, who's standing closest to the tree's base. "Camila, grab my hand, will you? I don't want to fall."

Camila looks at her. "Why? What's the worst that could happen, right?"

"Camila, seriously? Help me out here," Mariam pleads, and it's about more than getting down from the tree.

Camila doesn't.

Mariam sets her teeth. She attempts the jump on her own and makes it, too, but the sack catches on a branch and comes free from her shoulder. The entire bundle goes tumbling into the river, and yep, there are all the fruits, bobbing downstream on the current. Mariam watches them go from the shore.

The look of shock on Camila's face is almost worth it until Mariam sees everyone else's crumpling with dismay.

"Ugh!" Luci collapses into a grumpy pile on the ground. "I hate this place! I hate these trees and these vines and everything. Why is everything so hard all the time?"

"Maybe Mariam can tell you," Camila sneers.

That's the last straw, apparently, because Eun-Ji stands abruptly and says, "Enough! I don't know what's going on with you two, but you're going to make up. Go to that grocery store nearby, take a hike, I don't care. Just fix it." She pauses, then shakes her head, making a dismissive motion with her hands. "And don't come back until you've sorted it all out. We can't be fighting at a time like this."

She turns away and the others follow, leaving a bristling Camila with an emotionally exhausted Mariam.

"Come on, sweetheart," Mariam says. "You can yell at me while we get some soap and stuff. Maybe some more canned food." They're running low, now, and while the store has probably been pilfered beyond recognition, it can't hurt to look.

Mariam starts off at a trot.

Camila stares after her for a moment, then jogs through the brush to catch up. "Is that what you think? That I want to yell at you?"

"Well, you haven't spoken to me since last night, so I'm guessing you're pretty angry." Mariam shrugs, then jumps, because whoa, Camila explodes.

"Of course I'm angry!" She is yelling, though Mariam doesn't think it would be a good idea to point that out.

"You've been hiding important information from us this whole time, information that could've—"

"Could've what?" Mariam is tired. So very tired. All she wants is for things to be back to normal again. She wishes she'd never gone after the snake. She wishes her father had just disappeared into hell and let the rest of the world continue on, humid and green or otherwise. "What could we possibly have done? Forced my dad to become the devil? If we could even catch him, how would we do that? And you know, up until the last night, I didn't even know this whole thing was his fault. Was I supposed to read his mind?"

Camila is silent for a moment. "I don't know," she sighs. "This is too weird."

"Welcome to my life," Mariam muses, the corner of her mouth crooking up in a smile despite herself.

Camila laughs, a genuine, honest to God laugh, and Mariam dares to hope. It almost feels like normal, but then Camila shuts down and they're back to the uneasy silence that's been plaguing them for the past few days.

Mariam's voice is gentle when she asks, "What would you have done in my place?"

"Oh, Mariam." And the way Camila says her name makes Mariam want to dissolve. "I just wish you'd trusted us."

Mariam takes a deep breath, lets it out again. "Camila, it's not that I don't trust you. It's just...I never told anyone what happened. No one, not even Ammu."

"Ammu?"

Oh, that's right. She never did explain just who Ammu was to her. "Ammu. My Uncle Aamir."

"Oh. Why not?"

Mariam pulls on the edge of her shirt, then decides. There's no point in keeping it all in now. She might as well tell Camila; it's not like the telling can make things any worse.

"Most of it happened when I was so little, I wasn't sure it wasn't just another nightmare at first. And when things started getting worse...when Daddy started getting more powerful and...weird, I just, I don't know. You're one of three people in the whole world who knows what happened, and to be honest, that's because you spied on the two people it happened to."

"I didn't spy!"

"Camila. It was eavesdropping at best."

The quiet stretches between them and Camila looks a bit sheepish. When she doesn't say anything, Mariam adds, "I want to trust you. I do trust you. I explained everything, didn't I?"

"It was like pulling teeth!"

"Yeah, but that's because it hurts to remember, Camila. It hurts a lot. I found my mother after she ate a fucking bullet, and then my dad summoned a Creature straight out of a horror film and made me shake Its hand. I was traumatized! I still have nightmares, Camila. I don't like to talk about it. Do you like to talk about losing your family?"

Camila shrugs, raises an eyebrow. "Yeah, actually. It makes me feel better."

"Well, I'm not like that. I'm just not. I met the devil, and It scared me. I was six years old, Camila. Six years old! Do you have any idea what the devil is like? It's terrifying, and It smells horrible, and Its hands are slimy, and Its voice. Camila, Its voice. It's like...like a thousand horrible nightmares laughing at you, and you can't say no. You just can't. And you saw what my dad is like. He wasn't like that before he met that Thing. He was warm and kind of a big teddy bear, and now he's this creepy...I don't even know! He doesn't care that his actions have killed people! He's not even human anymore. He thought he could control It, but he couldn't. It used him, and now my dad isn't my dad anymore, and..."

It's too much. Her father's news, Camila's stoniness over the past few days, rehashing her painful childhood, talking about her dad: it's too much. She trips over her breaths and they come too fast; she's getting lightheaded.

Camila is silent but then wraps her arms around Mariam and murmurs in her ear, "Slow down, Mariam. You need to breathe more slowly."

She repeats the words and squeezes Mariam tight until she finally calms down. She still feels like her head is full of helium, but her breathing stabilizes.

Camila steps away from her. "I'm sorry. Maybe I've been unreasonable, but it's a lot for anyone to take in."

Mariam lifts up her hands. They're shaking, she realizes.

God. She's so pathetic.

Camila reaches out and enfolds Mariam's trembling fingers in her own. They're warm and Mariam can't help but hold on.

"I'm sorry," Camila says again.

"Me too."

They stand in silence a moment, but it's a different kind this time, and after a while, Mariam asks, "We good?"

"Give me some time. I just need to think. But I'll stop being so..."

"Hostile?"

Camila winces. "Yeah."

It's more than Mariam had expected but less than she'd hoped for. Looks like this will just have to do.

Chapter Nine

AT THE GROCERY store, Camila and Mariam venture into the back rooms. There aren't any canned goods out front, where everything is either missing, rotten, or trapped under the remnants of the roof, but maybe no one has thought to sneak a peek behind the doors in the back.

It turns out to be a brilliant idea, and afterward, neither girl can remember who came up with it; all they know is they've hit the jackpot. There are so many canned goods that they don't even have the space in their packs to take the boxes upon boxes back. As usual, Mariam looks for anything edible left from the "world foods" section, anything to bring some flavor to their meals. She would kill for cumin, a spice of any kind, really. But as usual, nothing salvageable. There are canned mandarins, though, and it's Camila who makes the discovery with a cry of delight. Maybe they'll have oranges for dessert after all! They decide to come back later and are so buzzed by the find that Mariam almost forgets to grab some soap.

The first leg of the walk back is miserable. Their packs are heavy, and the heat and humidity make their labor more difficult than it has to be. For once, Mariam wishes it was raining. Then she thinks better of it and rescinds the wish, sending vibes to whatever god is still listening to her that no, please just no more rain.

They talk on the way a little, about nothing important, but it's good. Pleasant. Camila is looking at her without any of her recent ire, at least, and they even have a laugh when a moth the size of Camila's fist lands on her nose. Suffice it to say that Camila hates bugs, but Mariam shoos it away, and soon they're trekking through the green again.

They're almost back to the cave when a high-pitched cry startles them out of their easy camaraderie. It...it sounds suspiciously like Carlos.

When it filters through the trees again, louder this time, Mariam and Camila look at each other for a moment before bolting in the direction of his screams.

"Carlos? Carlos, where are you?" Camila calls, desperation making her voice crack.

They hear a distant, "Camila!" in reply, and plunge deeper into the brush. Mariam wishes they'd taken the time to get rid of their packs, because man, this thing is seriously slowing her down.

The trees open up in front of them, and there's Carlos, his limbs tangled up in an oozy web of vines. He's struggling, glasses askew, and Mariam can see the marks on his skin where the sap has burned him. Camila starts forward, but Mariam snaps out her hand to hold her back. Something is moving in the mass of vines between them and Carlos—no, the mass of vines between them and Carlos is moving. It heaves and roils, hissing as the vines slide against one another, and then it's not just a pile of vines anymore. The center rises up, a tangle of moss and earth studded with those bulbous purple fruits that always strike Mariam as somehow sinister. They look like eyes. The thickest vines undulate around this center, and the whole creature resembles nothing more than a giant, vegetal spider. Okay, she knew this place was weird, but this? This is beyond bizarre, not to mention terrifying.

Uh oh.

The vine-spider's jaw opens up and it roars, bobbing and weaving in front of them. Next to her, Mariam feels Camila freeze up and stop breathing.

"Camila, focus!" Mariam whispers, just in case the creature can understand. "You get Carlos. I'll distract this thing."

Camila nods, and Mariam bursts forward like a cannonball, light on her feet and baiting the thing, hatchet held high.

It opens its mouth wide to roar, and the distinctive perfume of rotten fruit invades her nostrils, like it has before, like it did in the study when she was little and, oh. If her father hadn't put the pieces together for her, everything would have clicked into place at this very moment.

The vine-spider lashes out at her with a moss-furred leg, and she barely manages to dodge it. But dodge it she does, and she twirls and ducks and ignores the acid burns of the vines attacking her, ignores the heat and her labored breathing, the heaviness of her pack. She just has to distract this thing a little while longer so that Camila—

She hears a "Got him!" and turns to look. It's stupid, just a really stupid move. In that single moment of distraction, the great monster's maw wraps around Mariam's hatchet-wielding arm. She screams, pulls, and with a squelch, her arm is gone.

For the first second there is nothing, but in the next, searing pain hits her so hard she almost falls to her knees. It hurts. It hurts more than anything has ever hurt in her life, but she manages to run, following Camila and Carlos into the trees even as dark spots start swimming in her vision.

When it's safe, when they've stopped running, Mariam collapses. Her chest heaves and she chokes on her own tongue. It's then that Camila takes note of Mariam's missing arm, and her horrified intake of breath does nothing to assuage Mariam's panic.

"Carlos," Camila says, her tone unnaturally high, "Carlos, take your shirt off."

"But Camila," Carlos says, his voice a whisper, as though he hopes Mariam won't hear, "Mariam's arm is gone."

"That's why I need your shirt. Trust me, Carlos. And run back to camp, now. We need Ishmael."

Carlos obeys, stumbling back to their little encampment. They can't be far because not ten minutes after Camila's taken Mariam's pack from her shoulders and turned Carlos's shirt into a tourniquet, there's Ishmael.

There's no explanation needed. He picks up Mariam's pack, picks up Mariam, and carries them both into camp, Camila trailing behind like a lost puppy.

AS ISHMAEL CARRIES Mariam back into the cave, Eun-Ji bundles up some of the blankets to make her a bed. Camila grabs their little first aid kit from its home near the fire, runs to Mariam's side and drops to her knees, fumbling at the latch.

"D-don't bother. Save it for Carlos," Mariam hisses through clenched teeth.

"Don't give me any of your self-sacrificing bullshit right now, Mariam!" Camila is frantic, shaking as she pulls out bandages and ointments and other useless items.

Mariam can see why; she can feel why, but she also remembers the one thing Camila seems to keep forgetting. She can't die. That's the reason they're all in this mess in the first place.

"Camila, stop. S-stop. Carlos. He needs it. I don't." It hurts so bad. She wants to give in, fall into unconsciousness, but she needs them to understand, first. Take care of Carlos. Make sure they're all safe.

Camila listens for once, and the tears that have threatened since she discovered the loss of Mariam's arm finally drip from her eyes.

"I can't just sit here and do nothing! I need to help." There's snot running down her upper lip, and Mariam gets the absurd urge to laugh. Camila is an ugly crier. Instead, she gives a forced smile and brushes her remaining hand against Camila's damp cheek.

"I need water. Get me some water and I'll be fine." It takes all of Mariam's effort to keep her expression neutral, and the second Camila runs to accomplish the tasks set for her, her face collapses into anguish.

Eun-Ji makes a comment that's meant to cheer her up, something about how she'd sent them off to make up, not to kill each other. Mariam manages a weak laugh, then grimaces. A wave of nausea rolls through her and she dry heaves.

Oh God, oh God, she hurts so bad.

Maybe this is what her father meant when he offered to take away the hurt. He was trying to spare her this. Well, it didn't work. There's always a catch.

"S-someone needs to clean Carlos's b-burns," she manages, and Eun-Ji comes quietly to her, picks up the scattered first aid items Camila left and puts them back in the little kit. She looks like she's about to say something, but changes her mind and goes to tend Carlos's hurts.

From outside, she hears Hana trying to come in, and Luci trying to distract her. Their voices come to Mariam as if through glass. Someone somewhere is whimpering, and it takes her a while to realize that it's herself.

She's fading, but now here's Camila holding a water bottle to her lips. Her hands must be shaking, or maybe it's Mariam who's shaking because it gets everywhere before she manages to swallow any. For a second, the cool liquid on her tongue is distraction enough, and she smiles up at Camila through the red sparks of pain that are flashing behind her eyes.

"I'm good, Camila," she croaks, her voice a hoarse rasp. Then she's falling, straight down through the floor and into an inky blackness that she sinks into with thanks.

THERE'S LIGHT FLICKERING just past her eyelids, an inconstant glow that sends fizzles of jagged heat up into her brain. Sensation returns to her slowly, first a tingling in her feet, the tip of her nose, the scratch of the worn blankets on her skin. And then—

She gasps and lurches upright, stomach rolling again with the pain that's washing afresh through her arm, her arm that isn't there but somehow still is.

A hand presses her back down, gentle, and Ishmael's rumbling voice says, "Easy. Easy, Mariam. I've got you."

She sinks back into the wad of blankets he's made to prop her up, and almost allows unconsciousness to reclaim her. He's still talking, though, and she makes the effort to listen.

"...some food if you want it, just the usual corn and tuna. Those little mandarins you and Camila brought back too if you feel like dessert."

Maybe he's expecting her to reply and maybe he isn't, but she shakes her head anyway, just a little twitch left and right. There's the sound of a tin plate scraping on the asphalt floor.

"Yeah, figured you wouldn't be very hungry," he says. Then he pauses, and she cracks an eye open to see him looking uncharacteristically pensive.

"You know," he finally says, "I don't remember much from right after I lost the leg, and after a while, you probably won't either. It passes. This is the worst part."

Mariam grunts and she means it to be polite, a thank you, but honestly, she's still not quite all there and she's not sure he gets the message.

"Oh, I guess...I guess that might not make sense to you. Maybe you don't, ah...I wasn't born like this." He shifts, tugging up his pant leg. Mariam can't see what he does next, but she suspects he's taking off his prosthesis. When it's done, he holds it up for her to look.

"It was—an accident at work, all that machinery, you know? A split second thing. I was helping build—well, it doesn't really matter. That day, the days after were pretty bad, but honestly it was really about having to learn how to walk again." He pauses once more and glances at her shoulder. "There are a lot of things that you'll need to learn how to do again, I can guarantee you that, and not just physical things. It takes getting used to, having fewer limbs. And it's hard, I won't lie. It's really—" He lowers his voice to a whisper like he's afraid the kids will hear. "—really fucking hard. But you'll do it. You're a survivor; we all know that already. And, uh, if you want...if you need it, I'm here for you. For support."

He finishes with a look of embarrassment on his face, and Mariam grimaces. A twist of something, guilt, maybe, adds to her discomfort. He's just made himself very vulnerable to her, this gentle kind man, and how does she tell him it's all unnecessary? That her arm will grow back, that this is only temporary. Will he resent her?

He misinterprets the grimace. "It hurts like a bi—a lot doesn't it."

"That's not it," she manages through clenched teeth, though yes, yes it does hurt, and she has to take a few controlled breaths before she can continue.

"It...it might grow back." She decides the qualifier will make it easier to digest. She knows it'll grow back, or at least, she's pretty sure of it. Her dad lost a finger once after the deal, and that grew back. She sees no reason why her arm shouldn't, though regrowing bone, muscle, and tendon will take a little longer than healing skin, and it'll probably hurt like hell.

The look on Ishmael's face is hard to bear.

"What?" he says, slowly, and it's not resentment, but doubt in his voice.

"I...I think my arm might grow back." She doesn't add that the process will suck and hurt as much as losing it did in the first place. She doesn't add that she's not as sure of it as she sounds, because, oh God, what if it doesn't? What if it just heals over, and she loses her right arm? The thought opens up a chasm of fear in her mind, and she snaps it shut. Best not to go down that particular line of thought.

Pain flares, and it must show because the confusion on Ishmael's face shifts into concern. "Well, regardless of whether it does or doesn't, I'm here." She can tell he doesn't quite believe her but is grateful that he lets it go.

Ishmael takes the food, stands, and leaves Mariam to slip into a fevered sleep.

LAUGHTER, HUNDREDS OF laughing voices, but it's only one, only many.

"Come here, little girl. I'm waiting for you." The voice beckons, and she's drowning, drowning in a sentient darkness that wants to consume her.

Why is he doing this? Why does he keep bringing that Thing back, back to eat her dreams?

"Please! Stop bringing It here! Please, Daddy, why do you keep bringing It back?" Pounding the floor in anguish, pounding hearts screaming. Her hand is tingling, the invisible brand burning again like new, but now it's gone down another beast's belly.

Fear, bigger than the sea, bigger even than the whole world. "Stop it! Stop it!"

"Mariam," her father is trying his best.

"SHUT UP. I hate you. I hate you so much."

Explosions in the dark, colors burst, fireworks behind her bruised eyelids; Daddy shifts. He's changing, never himself for more than a moment. "I only ever did this to protect you, Mariam."

Chapter Ten

SHE WAKES UP from the fever-dream in the dark of the cave to find herself covered in a cold sweat. Lying limply next to her is a short appendage where her arm should be, and maybe it even resembles an arm a bit, except it's pink and swollen and a little bit sticky, and it looks more like it belongs to an overgrown fetus than to an eighteen-year-old girl. It's aching, too, not as much as the residual limb had ached, but it's definitely hurting more than most healing does. She pokes at it, and ow, it's sensitive. Moving it takes more effort than it should, and when she finally is able to make it do more than twitch, it jerks upward, almost hitting her in the face.

"Ugh, you'd better not stay like this forever," she mutters after the shock has subsided.

Something stirs on her left side, and oh! Camila? Yeah, it's her. Mariam lifts her good hand and rests it on Camila's stubbly head. The other girl mutters, "No, the sink is leaking," as she nuzzles into Mariam's touch. It's so nice to hear Camila sleep-talking, so normal, that Mariam almost laughs out loud. She refrains, sucking in a breath and smiling instead.

She really likes this girl, she admits to herself. She knows the fact that they've been thrown together in a high-stress environment has something to do with it, but she doesn't really care, except...she is in so much trouble because once Camila sees her arm is getting better, she's going to remember that she can't get hurt, and why, and then she's going to be mad at Mariam all over again.

The thought keeps Mariam from finding her way back to sleep, and she watches the forest outside their cave grow lighter as the sun rises.

OUT OF COURTESY or by some quiet pact they've made, the others leave her and Camila alone in the cave after they wake, creeping out to begin preparations for breakfast with only a few curious glances in their direction. Camila is still asleep, at least until the smell of warmed-over spam reaches their noses. Then Camila groans, stretches, and knocks her clenched fist into Mariam's head.

"Ow! Careful, sweetheart!"

Camila freezes midstretch, then scrambles sideways. "I'm so sorry. Are you okay? Oh my God, Mariam, I am so sorry. Did I hurt you?"

Mariam rubs her nose with her good arm and blinks to clear her watering eyes. "I'm okay."

The silence between them is uncomfortable, and Camila fills it with an equally uncomfortable question. "Your arm. Ishmael said it might...is it...um, you know?"

Mariam motions to her right arm, if it can even be called that, and shrugs. "I'm not sure."

Camila leans over to her see, so Mariam gets a good view of the surprise that plays out over Camila's face before she says, "Oh wow. Wow, that's incredible. I didn't think your regeneration abilities—I mean, I knew they were intense, but this is, wow."

"Yeah, I guess," Mariam says, relieved that Camila doesn't seem to be upset. But maybe it's just the shock.

Maybe it's coming. She doesn't get her hopes up until Camila sidles up next to her good side and laces their fingers together.

Then, Mariam can't help herself. She grins. "Whatever happened to needing time?"

Camila blushes, as always. Mariam is learning to really like that blush. "Yeah, well...I changed my mind. What you did for Carlos, and...I was so scared, Mariam. I mean, I know you can't die, but you looked like you could. You looked like you were going to and there was so much blood..." She trails off, shakes her head. "And I realized I couldn't lose you, not to a giant spider-freak and not to my own stubbornness. So there."

It's Mariam's turn to go red. "Wow, princess. Way to get deep," she says, maybe a little louder than necessary. But then she smiles, squeezes Camila's hand in hers, and says, gentler, "I wouldn't want to lose you either, you know?"

Neither of them really know what to say next, so Mariam just leans her head on Camila's shoulder and the two of them sit listening to the distant sounds of the others outside. Mariam has almost drifted back into sleep when Camila shifts a little.

"That was Eun-Ji calling me," she says, apologetic. "You rest. I'll be back later."

Mariam nods, only half awake, and settles back onto her nest of blankets. Sleep comes easy this time.

THEY COME TO her one by one throughout the morning, like pilgrims to her shrine, or so she likes to think of it. Ishmael shuffles over to raise his eyebrows at her new appendage, then grins and shakes his head. He brings her some mandarins, too, and they eat the sweet fruit together while laughing at the way her arm twitches when she wiggles her toes.

Eun-Ji visits not long after. She doesn't say much, only asks if she can do anything to ease the pain.

Mariam starts to shrug, then aborts the motion when it sends twinges of discomfort down her arm. "You're already doing a lot. Don't worry about me."

"Oh, I always do," Eun-Ji says. And with that, she's gone.

Luci comes with an offering of opam from that morning's breakfast, which Mariam eats gratefully as Luci tries not to stare at her arm.

And there's Carlos, who walks in with his arms all wrapped in bandages, his eyes wider than wide behind his glasses.

"Your arm's back," he says, and there's wonder, and maybe a little fear, in his voice. "It was gone. I saw it." He may be young, and he may not quite know what oranges are, but he knows that arms don't just regrow overnight. Or at least, they shouldn't.

"What did Eun-Ji say about it?" Mariam asks. She isn't sure how much Carlos knows, or should know. Best leave that to Eun-Ji's wisdom.

"She said you're lucky. She said you're special."

Well, those are two words she wouldn't pick out herself, but it'll work, for now.

"Yeah, I'm pretty lucky," she says and changes the topic before she has to explain more. "How are you feeling, buddy? Must have been scary in that web thing."

"I wasn't scared!" Carlos puffs out his chest, then deflates slightly. "Okay. Maybe a little. I wanted to go with you and Camila to the grocery store! I just wanted to help."

"Next time we'll go together, okay? No more wandering off on your own."

"Okay."

Then it's Hana's turn. "Hey, baby," Mariam says, her smile crooked. She really hopes her arm doesn't freak Hana out, but the chances of that are slim to none. Her arm is freaking her out.

"Hi," the little girl says shyly, shuffling her feet together. "Eomma said your arm got hurt saving Carlos. Can I see?"

Ah, well. She never could deny Hana anything to begin with. "Sure. I can't really move it, but," she uses her chin to point. "It doesn't really look like an arm, does it?"

Hana peers at the appendage, and answers, "It looks weird. Like a big worm."

Mariam can't help but laugh. "Yeah, it does!"

"Can I touch it?"

"Better not, sweetie. It hurts a lot."

"Oh. Okay. Can I sit in your lap?"

"If you're careful."

Hana crawls into her lap with uncharacteristic care, and Mariam wraps her good arm around the child.

"I love you a lot. Thank you for saving Carlos. I love him, too." Hana says, closing her dark eyes and resting her little head against Mariam's breast.

Mariam is touched. No one has said they loved her since Mom died. Dad and Amir loved her, sure, but they weren't vocal about it. They showed her in actions, but it would have been good to have had that confirmation from them. Anyways it's nice, really nice, but she doesn't know quite what to say. She settles with a "thank you."

"Don't you love me?" Hana asks, looking up through her thick lashes with the beginnings of a pout growing on her mouth.

Mariam opens her mouth, closes it, then gives a wavering smile.

"Yeah, baby. Yeah, I love you."

AFTER THEY'VE ALL come and gone, Camila sits beside her and takes out the book that she'd found in that house all those weeks ago. Its faded blue cover is a little worse for wear, now, spotted with damp and going slightly green at one corner, but the pages inside are dry and smooth. Camila runs her fingers reverently over the spine before speaking.

"Do you mind if I read a little bit to you?"

"Go ahead." Mariam glances at the cover and starts a bit. Well, she hasn't seen that in a while. "Interesting pick," she says.

"I always loved A Little Princess. Have you ever read it?"

"Hello? The girl without a mom and an absentee dad? Only about a million times."

Camila laughs. She opens the pages and gets a few words in when Hana stirs from her nap and sits up, popping her thumb out of her mouth. She catches sight of the book and grins.

"I wanna hear!" she demands, crawling towards them and situating herself on Camila's lap. "Start again!" Hana ponders a moment, then adds a sheepish "please."

Camila's lips twitch in what Mariam can only guess is amusement. She's about halfway through the first page when Carlos wanders in, grass clinging to his clothes and bandages. "I'm bored. What are you doing?"

Camila sighs. "I'm trying to read."

"You have a book? Is it the one about dinosaurs?"

"That one was left when—" Camila pauses. "—we left it in our old camp, the one before we met Mariam. This one is A Little Princess."

Carlos scrunches up his nose.

"Is there kissing?"

"No. It's about a girl your age, Carlos." Camila smiles indulgently.

Carlos frowns and considers, then nods. "Oh. Okay then. Can I listen?"

"Of course."

Camila has almost gotten to the second chapter when Luci comes in, her arms full of firewood.

"Whatcha reading?" She asks around the bundle, peering curiously down at their gathering.

Camila gives a tight smile and puts the book down in her lap.

"A Little Princess."

"Oh. What's it about?"

Mariam interrupts then, mock horror adorning her features. "You've never read A Little Princess?"

"Uh, no?" Luci raises an eyebrow at Mariam and Mariam throws her good hand into the air.

"This is a travesty. Luci, sit down. Camila, start again."

"I'm not starting again," Camila states flatly.

Mariam gives a cough and sticks her lower lip out in a pout. She even flutters her eyelashes for maximum effect. "But I'm sick. I'm sick, Camila."

Camila looks incredulous. "Don't you dare pull that on me, Mariam."

Mariam coughs again, causing her right arm to twitch violently. It gives a little squish as it flops back down to the ground.

"Fine, all right, just stop doing that!" Camila's mouth is twisted in annoyance and a hint of horror at the sight of Mariam's right arm. She snaps open the book again and flips to the first page as the others huddle around. Carlos leans against Camila's arm to get a good look at the pictures, and even though Luci sits next to Mariam with an air of affected disinterest, pretty soon she's as riveted as everyone else. Mariam closes her eyes and lets Camila read her back into a half sleep.

In the end, they only get to the second chapter before Eun Ji and Ishmael call everyone away to let Mariam rest, but it's all right. It's better with everyone, anyway.

THROUGHOUT THE DAY, her arm begins to lose its stickiness and elongates more, with a weird stretching feeling that half itches when it doesn't feel like it's been flayed. Mariam has a sneaking suspicion that a good chunk of the healing is going to happen during the night, and hopes that by tomorrow, it'll be back to normal. She's already regaining some more mobility, and that's nice.

It's not until after dinner that Mariam finally feels well enough to venture out into the forest, and even then, she stays close to the overpass. She isn't in any shape to really defend anyone, including herself right now. Besides that, her hatchet's gone, down the stomach of the spider-thing, assuming it even had a stomach. She supposes she could always try to go back and find it, but nah. Better not. The hatchet had a good run while it lasted, and she doesn't want to push her luck.

Camila finds her loitering a little ways away from the camp, sitting on a log.

"Hey," she offers.

"Hey," Mariam replies.

It feels like there's always too much silence between them, too many awkward moments and pregnant pauses, and wow, there's something heavy about this one. Mariam isn't sure what's going on. She thought they'd mostly sorted it all out, but Camila is looking at her with intention and purpose.

She sits down, and Mariam is panicking because whoa, suddenly she's realizing maybe Camila isn't mad at her at all. They weren't even talking yesterday, and she thinks Camila's about to—

Yeah. Their lips meet, and it's tentative, just a brushing of mouths. Camila pulls back shyly, but then Mariam closes the distance between them again because oh, kissing Camila is all she's wanted for such a long time. She parts her lips, plucks at Camila's, and Camila responds in kind.

Mariam's left hand reaches up to cradle Camila's jaw, and Camila makes a little noise that sends tingles down Mariam's spine. It's sweet, so sweet, and it feels good and nice and wow, kissing Camila is like that song, the closest to heaven that she'll ever be, even if they are in the middle of the apocalypse.

They part again, and Camila's eyes are closed, her lips pursed as though she wants more. Mariam wants to give her more, wants to shower her with kisses and let her hand wander down Camila's neck.

They hear a shout, Eun-Ji calling for them to come in, and Camila twitches away.

"We should..."

"Yeah."

Mariam can feel from the heat in her face that she's blushing to match Camila, but she doesn't mind, especially not when Camila takes her hand and leads her back to the overpass.

Chapter Eleven

MARIAM HAD HOPED that once they'd gone to bed, there would be more kisses. After all, they're tucked up in their own little corner of the cave, her and Camila, far enough from the others to feel some illusion of privacy. When Mariam tries, though, Camila shakes her head. She worries she's done something wrong, and the panic must show, because Camila's eyes dart to where Eun-Ji and Hana are talking quietly, to Carlos and Luci already sleeping by the fire. Oh! Yeah. Discretion. She may have forgotten about that.

But who could blame her? She just wants to kiss her girlfriend—wait. This is so new, they haven't even talked labels yet. Not that she doesn't want to because, but well, it's not...it's complicated. You can't just ask someone if they want to be exclusive when the world is falling apart, even if their kisses are really nice. Besides. It's not like there's an abundance of people their own age. Who else is she competing with, anyways? The only other humans they run into these days are in varying stages of decomposition.

"What are you thinking about?" Camila asks, her eyes boring into Mariam's. Mariam blinks.

"Uh. I was just, you know. Thinking about my dad," she lies, because really. She does not want to get into the whole girlfriend conversation right now. She doesn't want to pressure Camila into anything.

"Oh baby," Camila says, and Mariam's stomach lurches at the intimacy of it. Pet names always make her go kind of weak at the knees, and from Camila it just makes her want to giggle and release the shimmering bubble of joy welling up inside of her. Instead, she sighs. "Too bad we can't, you know."

"Tomorrow," Camila promises and leans over to kiss Mariam's cheek in consolation.

IN THE MORNING, Mariam wakes up to find Camila is gone and her arm is completely healed, though missing a lot of pigmentation. It looks really weird.

For as long as Mariam can remember, her light-brown skin has been punctuated with dark freckles. This arm, while basically the same tone as the rest of her body, is a blank canvas devoid of its normal constellations, and the muscles feel atrophied. Otherwise, it's fine, if a little unnerving to look at.

She stretches, flexes her new right hand, and groans. There's no force in the flexing, and her arm feels tired already. Looks like she'll just have to play it safe for a while.

She hears a yell, and then Hana's slamming into her knees. "Your arm is better!" she cries, wrapping her stubby arms around Mariam's legs.

"Yeah, it is," Mariam says, laughing. She reaches down with the arm in question and ruffles Hana's short hair.

"I'm happy!"

"Me too, kiddo."

CAMILA CONVINCES HER to tell Eun-Ji and Ishmael about her dad.

"Just in case something happens again and you're out of commission for a few days. What if he shows back up?"

"I don't know…"

"I think they have the right to know."

Mariam can't argue with that.

Camila's the one who takes them aside, says, "We need to tell you something important," and Mariam is the one who explains her father's role in the rainforest from hell situation. It's weird to hear herself say it out loud, to hear words like "summoned a demon" and "magical invulnerability" leave her tongue and burst in the still air of the cave between her and the others. In the back of her mind, Mariam chews on telling them about trying to give her dad up to the Beast. She decides against it, though. It doesn't feel like the right timing.

Eun-Ji listens quietly, her hands folded in her lap, but Ishmael takes to pacing about halfway through.

She stumbles through the part where everything horrible that's happened is her father's fault—the part about taking over the underworld and avoiding responsibility—but she gets through it. It's important that they know. At the end of it, Mariam gives a weak laugh, and says, "I know I sound absolutely out of my mind right now, but—"

Ishmael stops pacing and shakes his head. "Stranger things have happened, Mariam. The day before yesterday, a giant spider vine monster attacked Carlos and took off your arm. And then it grew back. I mean, yeah, it doesn't sound real, but what about any of this sounds real?"

Mariam shrugs, but then nods, and Ishmael continues, "But this is good information to have. We'll keep a lookout for your dad." He mutters under his breath, but Mariam hears anyway, "I'd like to give him a piece of my mind."

Eun-Ji asks a question that Mariam hadn't expected, though in hindsight, she definitely should have. "Is your dad a threat?"

"I...I don't know. I don't think so. He didn't mean for all this to happen. I mean, he doesn't care, but it wasn't intentional." Mariam rubs her forehead. "I don't know. So long as you aren't actively hurting me, I doubt he'll do anything."

"And this...Beast? What about him?" Ishmael asks.

"It... I guess? I mean, I don't know about that either. It's looking for me—for me and my dad—but honestly, I don't think there's anything we can do about that." Mariam doesn't mention the ritual, the flowers, or the incantation, but she doesn't want them mixed up in that anyway. If she's going to try again, they should be far, far away when she does.

Eun-Ji gives Ishmael a worried glance, and then thanks Mariam for telling them. "It's good to know what's going on. So, at this point, it looks like we have two options. We either let you stay with us and hope your father will protect us, too. Or we can split up and hope this Beast-thing doesn't punish us for being near you."

Ishmael rolls his eyes. "We're not leaving Mariam alone to cope with that thing. She isn't going anywhere."

Eun-Ji looks like she's about to argue, then thinks better of it. "Okay. Let's just hope her dad will protect all of us."

Mariam realizes that to Eun-Ji at least, she is still an outsider. She can't fault Eun-Ji's logic, though: She has her daughter to protect. Even so, it leaves Mariam feeling like her lungs are drowning.

MARIAM STILL CAN'T do much strenuous work, but she offers to go pick fruit since the kids have been getting tired of the canned stuff. It's almost dark by the time she turns back with her arms full of some sticky red fruits that she's pretty sure are not poisonous.

She's picking her way carefully over a tangle of drowsy vines when there's a slithery rustle behind her, and then a voice, saying, "Evening, sweetie."

She doesn't turn. She doesn't need to. Instead, she sighs, "Oh no, not you again. Please just go."

"Is that any way to speak to your father, Mariam?"

Ugh.

"What are you doing here?"

"I saw you had some trouble, earlier. How's the arm? Good as new? I'd ask for a thank you, but then, you've never been very good with your manners."

Mariam bristles and a few of the fruits pop in her grip, spilling sweet-smelling nectar over her fingers. Yes, her brand new fingers that she wouldn't have without her father's help all those years ago. Then again, there are a lot of things that wouldn't have happened without her father's help. It makes her mad. It makes her so, so mad.

She turns, and there he is, suit and tie and deranged eyes and all.

"Do you think I owe you for this?" she hisses. "Do you honestly think that anyone would thank you for what you've done?"

He considers, and she can see his mind, if he still has one, whirring through his options. Eventually, he settles with, "I should expect it from you, at least. You're here, you're...whole, because of what we did."

"What you did. What you made me do." Pop, pop, pop. There goes the fruit. She's shaking, her hands clenched around the remnants of her harvest even though her arm is numb and tingly from the effort.

Malik shrugs. Shrugs, like none of it matters, not her terrified six-year-old self, not the millions of people crushed in their homes and eaten by the earth, not the burns on Carlos's arms or the fact that Luci still cries herself to sleep at night.

Mariam trembles with the effort of keeping her voice even. "Let me tell you about a little kid named Nayara. I watched her bleed out on the ground. She had black hair and brown eyes and a big sister who's still grieving her, and she was ten. That's on you, Dad."

Perhaps a shadow crosses over Malik's face, but it's hard to tell in the dark, and, besides, he's not quite human enough for his expressions to mean anything definitive anymore.

"I thought the child would want a friend. I didn't mean for that to happen."

"What?"

Malik looks sheepish, but his shoulders rise and fall in another shrug. "She reminded me of you. She wanted a playmate. How was I to know the creature's parents would... For what it's worth, it wasn't on purpose."

"Oh my God." Mariam can feel the blood draining from her cheeks. The fancy man Hana had told them about. She's almost forgotten, it's been so long, but now it makes sense. She's about to yell, scream, something, when her father waves his hand.

"No need for hysterics. You want to blame me for this, that's fine," he says. "But I came to warn you."

"Warn me about what? What else could you have possibly done to screw things up any more than they already are?" She curses at him. It comes out more violently than she means, but then it really doesn't matter—he deserves it.

"Language, Mariam." He pinches the bridge of his nose between his fingers like her words have personally offended him. Good. Then, "It's not something I've done, or not quite."

Mariam waits. He stares at her with eyes that are too bright, too still.

"As I hinted earlier, I, ah, am avoiding making good on that deal at the moment. Delaying, if you will. There are some...consequences. The Beast—the Creature you met, before—is, was the steward of...hell, I suppose. The otherworld, the down below, whatever you want to call it. I agreed to take Its place in return for protecting you, and myself, but since I found that lovely little loophole...things have gotten a little tense. The Beast is refusing to do Its job, and there's hell to pay. Quite literally, without Its stewardship, hell is exceeding its boundaries. Bleeding into our world. That's why—" He gestures around to the forest. "—all this."

"Right, so everything is your fault, people have died and are dying because you refuse to take responsibility for your actions. Tell me what's new, again?" She's losing patience with him, as she usually does.

"Yes, well...there's more. Hell needs a steward. It wants to claim me, by whatever means it can. Thanks to your little trick with the flowers, the Beast has finally figured out you and I are in the area and...It's alerted the authorities. The powers that be. What I mean is, the landscape knows we're here, and it's out for blood. Yours.

Mine. Just be careful, darling. Wouldn't want any more accidents like the one with your arm, would we?" He ends with a smile that stretches the skin of his cheeks in a mockery of sincerity.

"Wait, you saw that?"

"More importantly, so did the Beast. What were you trying to achieve with that summoning anyways?"

Mariam ignores his question. "You mean...that spider thing, the thing that attacked Carlos...that was because of me?" Horror carves out an empty cavity in Mariam's chest, and she drops the rest of the fruits, arms going limp at her sides.

"It may have been the first, but it won't be the last. Like I said, just be careful." He pauses, and his smile grows again.

"I don't need your warnings or your help. I can take care of my people on my own!"

"Oh, Mariam. Why do you think you and your friends haven't encountered anyone else? Do you really think you're that lucky?" He sighs. "Suit yourself. But remember what I told you. I'll be nearby if you need me."

Mariam reaches out grab at his lapel, to hold him here and make him answer for everything, but he's already gone, faded into himself. There's a rustle in the undergrowth, but nothing more.

It takes her a while to realize what he means, to connect his words with the bodies they've met along the way, and when it hits her, she kneels to the ground and tries not to hurl.

Chapter Twelve

SHE DOESN'T TELL them. How could she? Instead, she lets it sit in the pit of her stomach, heavy and festering. Nayara, and the bodies, and how many more deaths is her father directly responsible for? The knowledge is a chain she carries with her, and every time they encounter more fresh dead, she has to force the sick back down her throat.

Worse still is knowing Carlos was attacked because of her; her actions almost got him killed. She tries not to think about it, but every so often she'll see Carlos trying not to scratch at his burns and looking at her regrown arm warily. She forces the thoughts from her mind and wonders if that makes her as bad as her dad.

Her father doesn't show himself again, but she's always looking, listening for that unsettling slither. When it doesn't come, Mariam begins allowing herself to relax. It isn't until a week after the encounter that he shows any signs of himself.

Mariam jerks awake to Hana's insistent tugs on her arm, groggy, with drowsiness still buzzing behind her eyes. The girl has pounced on her and Camila, tangled up together as they are in the blankets. Camila is, as usual, sleeping like a baby, only stirring to mumble her occasional dreamspeak.

"Mariam! Mariam, wake up! You said you'd teach me how to make flower crowns! I wanna learn! Eomma says we can go out and look for flowers today!"

Mariam sits up and rubs at her face. "Gimme a second, Hana. I need to wake up."

"But you're already up!" Hana bounces back onto her heels, crouching next to Camila's still-prone form and reaching out to give her arm a determined poke.

Mariam grimaces. "I miss coffee."

At that, Camila finally stirs. "Did I hear coffee?" she mumbles sleepily.

"Just wishing out loud, sweetie," Mariam laughs.

Camila groans and burrows her face in Mariam's lap. "Don't wanna get up yet," she grumbles.

"Flower crowns!" Hana yells and jumps up to begin running laps around their bedrolls.

Faced with Hana's exuberance, they drag themselves out of their blankets. Mariam is still not quite awake, and a lingering exhaustion dogs her throughout the morning, but soon, Hana's excitement infects them all.

All of the kids go, even Carlos, who spends the entire trek clarifying that he doesn't want a flower crown for himself, he just wants to keep watch. Sure, Carlos. They all need something to make their lives a little brighter anyway. Flower crowns worked so well the first time, and they'll be even better now that they aren't woven in with guilt, Mariam thinks. She's looking forward to the venture.

They find a clearing, smaller than the one where Mariam had tried her offering the first time, this one carpeted with a swaying field of pink flowers. Perfect for crowns: Hana's delighted. The kids settle down in the middle, and Mariam gets to work showing everyone how to weave the stems together.

Camila tries really hard, but she's not too good at the whole crafts thing. Even Hana, with her tiny little hands, gets it faster than Camila does, but no one can say she doesn't try. In fact, when she kind of succeeds, she sheepishly presents the lopsided crown to Mariam, who wears it proudly.

Hana is working on her second flower crown—"For Eomma!"—with her first one perched precariously upon her head, when she stills suddenly and cups a hand to her little ear.

"What's that?" she asks, not afraid yet, though perhaps getting there.

"What?" Mariam asks, but then she too hears it: a low hum, a rumble, like something is stirring beneath their feet, just like before, before everything went to hell—

Mariam grabs Hana and Carlos too, dragging them both along toward the trees and shouting for Camila and Luci to follow. By the time they reach the shaded ground under the branches, the ground is shaking and they stumble into one another. Mariam glances back over her shoulder just in time to see the meadow erupt into chaos, flowers disappearing under churning earth. There's a wrenching groan, inhuman and deep, and then—nothing. The ground beneath their feet goes solid and still.

"Is everyone okay?" Camila asks, glancing around at the kids. The others nod, too shocked, maybe, to have started to cry.

"Let's go home. We need to see if Eun-Ji and Ishmael are safe," Mariam says and starts to tug Hana up into her arms, but then the little girl is squirming and pulling away.

"My flowers! I need to give them to Eomma!" she cries and slips under Mariam's arm to run back into what used to be their meadow.

"Hana, come back, it's not safe!" Camila runs after her, and soon everyone follows, stomping over spongy earth to where Hana's stopped in the middle of the field.

"Look," she says as they catch up to her, pointing to something on the ground. "It came out of the dirt."

They all circle around the glittering metal of Mariam's hatchet returned to them from the belly of the beast.

Mariam picks it up hesitantly, finding the words "YOU'RE WELCOME SWEETIE" burned into the handle. A bloom of anger erupts in her chest, and her face must change to reflect it, because a hesitant Hana asks, "What's wrong, Mariam?"

Mariam considers casting it back to the ground, considers rejecting this gift the way she couldn't reject the healing when she was six. She almost does it too, but Camila stays her hand.

"We might need it," she says, quiet.

Mariam sighs, but nods and throws it over her shoulder. The handle is smooth and warm in her palm, and, yeah, there's a part of her that's glad to have its familiar weight back in her hands, passive-aggressive engravings be damned.

"C'mon everybody," she says, pulling her mouth into a tight smile. "Time to go back."

IT TAKES A couple of more days, but even with the hatchet beside her bed at night, she almost forgets her father's warning. Almost. The group falls into a routine of sorts, familiar if not quite comfortable.

Their overpass-turned-cave proves resilient against heat, rain, and anything else that might want to worm its way into their sleep. The grocery store is, for now, and the foreseeable future, a reliable source of food. The river frees them from the necessity of collecting rainwater, and its incessant tumbling roar lulls them into sleep when the silence of the forest would be too much, too quiet and too alive all at once.

Hedged into the group by Eun-Ji's quiet calm, Ishmael's easy strength, and nights spent reading to the kids and teaching them how to sing, Mariam allows her father's warning to shrink to an itchy knot at the very back of her brain, easy to ignore when there are so many other things—good things—to occupy her mind. Good things, like the way that Camila smiles at her across the fire, or the way her brown hair is growing back in tufty clumps that stick out over her pretty little ears.

There are smiles, and flower crowns, and kisses, and it's good; it's so good.

Until it isn't. Until the forest wakes up.

When it does, it happens fast. One day, Luci gets her foot trapped in a nest of vines that try to hoist her up into a tree until Eun-Ji hacks them to pieces with a utility knife, and her ankle comes away wreathed in bruisy purple and acid burns. The next, a horde of those same hyperintelligent monkeys chases Ishmael home from a trip to the abandoned grocery store. He comes back with claw marks covering his shoulders but still manages to bring them a pack full of canned soups, to his everlasting credit.

The whole forest is prickling with a sense of wrongness, of shadows that are too dark and full of eyes. Watching. The others might not feel it, but Mariam does, and it makes her shiver into the crook of Camila's shoulder at night. Camila thinks she's being paranoid, but

Mariam keeps a hand curled around her hatchet as she sleeps, rubbing a thumb over the lettered grooves.

No one can deny that the vines and even the other plants have been more aggressive of late, rearing up at the slightest provocation to seize and trip and burn. Eun-Ji doesn't let Hana or Carlos wander out of sight of the cave without a chaperone anymore. And then there's the issue of the vines around the cave, which have begun to creep ever closer, wrapping exploratory tendrils around the mouth as if contemplating an invasion.

The kids accept it all as part and parcel of their new, danger-around-every-corner lifestyle, but Mariam knows.

They're looking for her.

She grits her teeth and tries to ignore it for a few days, hoping that it'll blow over. Maybe it's all just a coincidence. Or maybe not, but perhaps her dad will decide to take up the mantle after all, and this god-awful place will just leave her in peace. Right.

Ignoring it becomes impossible when the forest comes for Hana. They're trekking back from the river, her and Eun-Ji and Hana and Camila, carrying the day's water when Hana veers off from their track to skip after a fluttery blue butterfly. She doesn't go far, just bouncing along parallel to them through a screen of trees and humming as she does when she's happy, which is most of the time, despite everything. Eun-Ji keeps a watchful eye but lets her have her fun. It's fine, and it's nice to see the kid enjoying herself. Until Hana just isn't there anymore.

The humming cuts out on a squeak and Hana vanishes. One second she's there and the next she's gone. Then there's a shriek, a high-pitched scream of "Eomma, Eomma help!" and they all three drop their buckets and plunge through the brush toward her voice.

A litany of no no no no no buzzes through Mariam's ears as she struggles through the vines. Her hatchet hacks open a path and she steps out into a clear space, Camila and Eun-Ji close behind. There's Hana, sunk to her tiny waist in the ground, which is undulating and rippling around her, a puddle of tar-black mud that couldn't have been there just a second ago welling up through the moss. She reaches out toward them then, face streaked with the stuff, and sinks farther. The butterfly floats away into the canopy, a pretty blue blur against the green.

"Hana!" The cry rips itself from Eun-Ji's throat and she jerks forward to grab for her daughter, but then she too is sinking, already mired up to her knees and falling fast. "Hana!" she cries again as Camila hauls her up onto solid ground, horror making a crack and a shiver of her voice.

They don't have time for emotions, though, even when panic is already lodged between Mariam's ribs, because it's Hana, it's tiny, precious Hana and the fear on that little face is heartbreaking.

"Hold onto me," Mariam orders, lifting her hatchet. Camila grips her proffered hand, and Mariam wades in, feeling the ground give way under her feet already. She's up to her waist and only halfway to Hana, who's flailing as best she can to keep afloat in the sticky ooze. It's lapping against her chin.

"Eomma!" Hana cries again and chokes on a mouthful of mud.

Mariam takes another swimming step and the sludge swallows her up to her armpits. She can feel it sucking at her feet, trying to draw her down into whatever putrid underworld lurks beneath the roots of the forest. Camila's grip on her sweaty wrist is slipping, so she flings out her arm and offers the handle of her hatchet to Hana. It has to reach. It has to be far enough. Please, let it be far enough.

"Hana, baby, I'm here, I've got you, okay? Can you hold onto this?" She asks as the blade of the hatchet bites deep into her palm.

Hana turns her panicked gaze toward her and Mariam can see her eyes are glazed with terror, but reach out she does, and Mariam feels a tug on the end of her axe. She's never been more grateful to her dad. You're welcome, sweetie indeed.

"Hold tight, baby. Camila, pull us up!"

She steps back as best she can, feeling Camila and Eun-Ji pulling on her arm from behind, and Hana dragging through the mud before her. It's a close thing, and for a second Mariam is pretty sure her new arm won't take the strain, which would suck in multiple ways, but then there's a sluuurrrpp and they're both tumbling back onto solid ground, into Camila and Eun-Ji's arms.

In front of them, the pool of sludge bubbles and stirs, angry that they've escaped its oozy grip.

Mariam scrambles to her feet with Hana clutched in her arms. "Let's go," she says.

They do, crashing through the forest without a thought for the vines snatching at their clothes and ankles, buckets abandoned. It isn't far to the cave, but it feels like forever. Mariam can feel Hana's heart fluttering against her breast like the world's most frightened little bird. She's still caked in mud and clinging to Mariam's neck, crying muddy tears and whimpering.

Finally, there's the cave; there's home. And there are those vines, oh god those freaking vines, how she'd like to rip them all up and set them ablaze. Mariam gives one cluster a vicious kick as she steps inside to lay Hana down by the fire. Eun-Ji's there in an instant to wipe the mud away from Hana's mouth, to cover her tearful face in kisses.

Mariam shucks some of the sludge off of her own arms and turns away, slipping the hatchet back into her belt.

This was too close. It can't happen again. There's a hollowness in her chest that even Camila's reassuring smile can't shake.

Third Interlude

IT FLEXES ITS fingers, feeling the joints pop and creak as the loose flesh rasps and flakes. It has favored this form for a long while now, since before time stopped meaning, so much so that it is easy to slip from the immaterial into this physical monstrosity, tall and gaunt and full of rot. It is terrifying, and that is how It likes it. All the better to greet these humans with, though sometimes It has wondered if a gentler approach would yield different results.

Humans are troublesome things. There is knowledge, somewhere in Its consciousness, that at some time It was not so different from these humans, with their quick, fragile breaths and fickle hearts. That was a long time ago, and the memory of flesh has long since disappeared. This—these hands of bone and the heaving, empty chest that It puts on for these forays into the living world—are Its only semblance of a body.

The ground beneath Its feet shivers as It walks, the vines shrinking away from Its steps and writhing in vegetable ecstasy in Its presence. All over this forest now It can feel Its tendrils of consciousness moving: slithering, pulsing, growing, digging in. It feels the girl and the remnants of her sacrifice too, a beacon in the tangled forest, the center of all this. It won't hurt her—not yet— not until she's desperate enough to do what needs to be done.

It sucks jungle air into ruined lungs, hot and humid and familiar, and sneers. Oh, what fools they all are.

Chapter Thirteen

MARIAM MAKES THE hard decision, the only thing she can do, because after a night of listening to Hana crying out from nightmares, her conscience can't take it. Worse, maybe, the vines at the mouth of the cave are getting closer, leaking their acid sap and smelling of sharp green, and she knows it's her fault.

Everything, it's all her fault, but she just can't leave. She can't do it, not on her own. She takes it to Eun-Ji and Ishmael early in the morning when everyone else is still asleep, leaving Camila curled up in their blankets. Mariam doesn't want her to influence this conversation.

"Eun-Ji, Ishmael. I need to tell you something."

Eun-Ji peers up at her with eyes sunken from the fear of almost having lost her daughter, and Ishmael just looks exhausted.

"Can't it wait 'til it's light out?" Ishmael asks.

This is my fault, Mariam thinks, steeling herself. She has to make this right.

"No. It can't."

Eun-Ji sighs, "All right," and pats the ground beside her.

Mariam doesn't sit, just stands before them and lets her hands clench and unclench themselves at her sides. The words stick in her throat for a moment, but she decides to lead with, "It's getting more dangerous because of me." It's not so much a confession, but it's a start.

"That's ridiculous, Mariam," Ishmael says, but Eun-Ji is looking at her with something that looks like calculation. It's easy to forget with all of Eun-Ji's gentle mothering that she's still a survivor, a survivor who'd give up the world for her daughter.

"What do you mean?" the older woman asks.

"You remember that whole thing about my dad and the Beast and all that? How the Beast was looking for us? Well, I... I maybe got Its attention, I think, and now..."

"What do you mean?" Eun-Ji asks again, and Mariam squirms under her scrutiny. Fine, she'll spell it out.

"I did the ritual. I was trying to get It to talk to me so I could tell It where to find my dad, but It never showed up. I gave It our location, basically. Everything that's been happening—Carlos, Luci, Hana and that mud pit—they aren't accidents. They're because I'm here, and because I was stupid."

Eun-Ji's eyes dart to where Hana is sleeping fitfully by the fire, even as Ishmael blinks in confusion. Then her eyes are back on Mariam, colder than they've ever been. It makes Mariam feel like crawling into a hole, disappearing, running away. Which, if she's honest with herself, would probably be the best solution after all.

But those eyes, those hard, cold eyes, soften when Ishmael says, "We all make mistakes. You were trying to look out for us. I mean, yeah, we would have appreciated being clued in, but we would've died a hundred times over without you to save the day. None of us would've made it out alive that first time we met if it wasn't for you and that axe of yours."

He's right. He's right, but he's also so wrong and the truth of that is eating at Mariam's insides. "You don't get it!" she whispers. "It knows I'm here now! It wants me—

maybe It doesn't want me dead, but It certainly doesn't want you all alive. This isn't going to stop. I'm too dangerous to have around." She looks down. She hadn't meant to tell them that, but now that it's out, there's nothing she can do. And maybe this'll make them make her go. She needs to go for them to be safe, and she needs the push.

They're silent, both of them, but then Ishmael stands. "We aren't going to abandon you, Mariam. We aren't. I can't say—" He swallows. "—I like what's going on. But we need you. And we want you to stay. But we need you to trust us, too. So, you need to let us know what's going on. No more keeping secrets." Oh, how those words must cost him.

Mariam opens her mouth to argue, then decides against it, because, really? She can't bear the thought of leaving them.

"I'll sleep outside," she tries. "The vines would probably back off."

"No. You're staying here, in the cave, with us," Ishmael says. But when Eun-Ji smiles in affirmation, it doesn't reach her eyes.

"Fine," Mariam says. "But the offer still stands. The second you decide it's too dangerous, just say the word and I'll go."

Ishmael shakes his head, but Eun-Ji just looks back at her, gaze steady. Mariam shudders under the weight of it.

SHE STAYS AND every morning hopes she'll wake to find things have returned to normal. Normal, she thinks with a humorless chuckle, meaning the extra-hellish jungle will transform back into a regular hell-jungle. Funny how things change.

It doesn't, though, and they adapt. It's too dangerous to venture far from the cave, even far enough to fetch water or forage for fruit, so Eun-Ji makes all of the kids stay inside. Hana doesn't mind. Hana hasn't been interested in going outside since the incident with the butterfly and starts to whimper whenever someone leaves the cave. She's afraid they won't come back, she says, tearful, and though the others do their best to reassure her, Mariam can't help but share her fear.

The forest wants them dead. She's certain of it, and so she volunteers to make the trips to the grocery store on her own, battling off sentient trees and the occasional monkey, leaping over sudden pitfalls and being careful where she steps. Interestingly enough, no tar pits, but that could change at any moment, she knows.

The forest gets her, sometimes, and she spends each trip painted in cuts and scrapes that sting as they close up. Once, a particularly vicious vine sent her sprawling and she had to curl in on herself to rock back and forth as her broken ankle slid back into alignment. It freaking hurt, but better her than them, right? It's the least she can do. She made sure she was all healed up before heading into camp again, and every time she comes home with a backpack full of food, she's far too relieved to find the others still alive, huddled in their blankets and watching the outdoors with eyes full of suspicion. She's brought this on them, and she can't decide if it's a sign of weakness or strength that she hasn't yet left to relieve them of her company.

The vines are creeping ever closer into their cave, shifting and slithering even during the day, and the only thing that seems to slow their determined invasion is the fire. They keep it stoked at all times now to keep the vines at bay, regardless of how hot it is outside. Mariam, Camila, Eun-Ji, and Ishmael take it in shifts at night to keep it from going out when the wind blows in gusts of warm rain.

It's hard to sleep without Camila when her shift to watch the fire comes up, but Mariam is so exhausted these days that she manages it. Besides, if Eun-Ji and Ishmael can do it, so can she. She wonders if it's as hard for Camila, but then she shakes the thought. It doesn't matter, not really. If things keep going the way they've been going, Mariam probably won't be welcome much longer.

Tonight is Mariam's turn, though, and as she's done every night, she watches the fire with her hand wrapped loosely around her hatchet, glancing every now and then at the dark shapes gathering outside their cave. But she's exhausted now, they all are, and this time her eyes droop until the flames bloom into flowers and twist into monsters and...is that screaming? A strangled cry reaches her through the fog of sleep. Her bleary eyes snap open and as she gazes into the sputtering light of the fire, she begins to understand that the blurs of motion at the mouth of the cave are Camila and Hana, dragged from their beds and suspended in the air by two thick vines circling their necks. Camila's fingers are scrabbling uselessly at her throat, face turning a terrifying shade of gray, and Hana mouth is gaping open like she's trying to scream, her small figure casting a puppet-like shadow on the walls.

Mariam blinks, and the severity of the situation hits her. Her exhaustion dissipates.

She grabs her hatchet and sprints for the entrance, cutting away at the vines that have pulled Camila and Hana toward the mouth of the cave, away from the fire. Mariam's so, so angry.

"Leave them alone!" she screams, and at the edges of her sight, she notes that the others are starting to wake up too. Carlos's voice starts up in a terrified wail, and then there's Eun-Ji at her elbow, tugging at Hana's arm and crying and crying.

Mariam's priority right now is to get them out of the vines and breathing again, but then Hana goes limp, and Camila isn't far behind. Mariam hacks at the base of the vines, tearing at them until, finally, Hana drops into Eun-Ji's arms and Camila falls to the floor, the snake-like plants slithering away into the dark.

Camila is still for a second but then breathes, crying and shaking as Mariam holds her. Her face is going back to its normal shade, even as the whites of her eyes are red and the burn marks on her neck flare up, shiny and dark.

Eun-Ji's got Hana lying on her back, hunched over her daughter to give her CPR, and for the seconds that nothing happens it feels like the whole world is holding its breath, even as Camila's gasps fill the overpass. But then Hana's little body convulses and she's choking, and Mariam feels the tension in the cave dissipate at least a bit.

"We need the first aid kit," Mariam hears herself say, and Ishmael is distributing gauze and alcohol packs to both Mariam and Eun-Ji before she even finishes her sentence.

"Mariam," Camila croaks, and then she's sobbing into Mariam's shoulder, her arms around Mariam's neck.

"I was so scared. I was so scared," she mouths out, her voice just a suggestion of a croak.

"I know, sweetheart, I know. I'm so sorry. I'm sorry. It's fine, everything's fine, now."

Except it's not. It hasn't been fine for a long time.

Later, when Ishmael has stoked the fire up to a crackling roar and installed himself and his shotgun between it and the night, Mariam runs her fingers gently along Camila's cheek. The girl is sleeping, now, her breathing wheezy from the bruises and burns that ring her throat. Occasionally she mumbles, as she has done every night since Mariam met her, and not for the first time, Mariam wonders what kinds of dreams are flickering behind Camila's closed eyelids.

Bad ones, tonight, if the crease in Camila's brow and her clenching fingers in Mariam's shirt are anything to judge by. Camila's mouth opens and she groans, says, scratchy, "...afraid. Wanna go home."

IN THE MORNING the vines are still there, quivering just past the shadow of the cave. There's no mistaking it anymore: they're alive and they want blood. Mariam gives the thickest ones a few good hacks as she steps over them into the dim morning sunlight. She's out to find more firewood, a small atonement for last night if that's possible. How could she have fallen asleep? The only thing she can do for them and she—there's a rustle behind her in the trees, and Mariam spins, ready to fight off whatever fresh antagonist the forest is going to throw at her.

It's only Eun-Ji, except maybe that's not all that different because the anger bunched on Eun-Ji's brow is a lot more frightening than anything she's seen leaping at her out of the trees.

"We need to talk, Mariam," she says, quiet and level but with a hardness that cuts.

Mariam holds up her hands in some kind of supplication. "Eun-Ji, Eun-Ji, I'm so sorry. I never should have—it won't happen again, I promise. I was just so tir—"

"Go."

The quiet word falls heavy in the air between them, and Mariam hears, but she doesn't want to hear, so she asks, "I'm sorry?"

Eun-Ji hesitates for just a second. Just a second, and then, "Leave. Please leave, and don't come back."

All the weight drops out of Mariam's chest and she's hollow, suddenly. Light, made of nothing. It's easy to walk back into the cave, easy to gather up her things, easy to ignore the sleeping forms of the others and go back out into the forest. Eun-Ji is there in the clearing, watching her with something Mariam doesn't care to read on her face. It's easy until she's turned her back on them all and pushes her way into the brush.

Then it's hard. So she starts to run.

Chapter Fourteen

SHE RUNS UNTIL gulping breaths of the humid air becomes too difficult, and stops to rest against a tree. Ddespite the way her eyes are still blurred with tears, she nevertheless remembers to check for the red, angry beetles that live just under the bark of most trees in the area.

The ground at the base of the trunk is mercifully clear, just carpeted with a spongy moss that is probably full of worms, so Mariam lets herself crouch there and lean her head down on her arms. Just for a moment, she thinks, but it must have been longer, and she must have been more tired than she thinks because when Camila comes crashing through the brush, the sun has risen enough to begin steaming the jungle and everything inside it.

"What are you—?" Mariam starts, but Camila holds up her hand and flings herself down next to Mariam on the ground.

"I saw what happened," she croaks, breathlessly. "Eun-Ji sent you away. You can't actually go. She's being unreasonable."

Mariam bites her lip and motions to Camila. "Look at yourself, sweetheart. You're covered in burn marks and, I mean, your throat. It looks like something tried to hang you. I mean, something did try to hang you. Your eyes are all red and you can't even talk right! It's horrific. I know we don't have mirrors, but trust me, it doesn't look good. Hana can't look much better, and Eun-Ji had every right to—"

"It looks better than being dead would. You saved my life! You saved Hana's too, twice in as many weeks. We're alive, thanks to you!"

"Camila—"

"No! Of course you fell asleep. You've been exhausted and getting food when no one else can and you're pushing yourself too much. I'm alive, Mariam. I'm here because you—"

"The forest is coming after us because of me." Mariam can't stand to have Camila tell her how great she is when she knows the truth.

"We already knew that."

"No, its... I... I tried to summon the Beast. That Thing I told you about. I basically, I sent out a homing beacon telling everything where we are. Carlos being attacked, Hana almost drowning, and the vines, they're all because I was stupid."

"What?" Camila looks confused, and she shakes her head. "Why would you try to summon that Thing?"

"Because! I wanted to take It to my dad. I wanted to make sure It knew that I had nothing to do with this, and neither did any of you. But it didn't work! I just... I almost killed all of you."

Camila chews her tongue for a long moment. Her hands make their way to her head, and she pinches at the short hair there before setting her jaw.

"That was really stupid of you. I'm kind of mad," she says eventually. "So, what now?"

"What do you mean, what now? Eun-Ji doesn't want me back, and you know I'm dangerous. I was just going to...I don't know, find my own cave or something. Live out my days fighting off sentient trees."

"What?" Of all the weird things she's said, this seems to bother Camila the most. She's half risen into a crouch and is glaring at Mariam—or trying to. The vines' acid seems to have burned off half of her eyebrow. "You've got to do something. Mariam, we've got to make it right."

Mariam would love to match the cold enthusiasm in Camila's face, but she's tired, and she already tried and failed. Can't they just stop?

"What else can we do? I told you, summoning the Beast didn't work, I—"

"Have you done it before? You must have seen It, with your dad?" Camila is looking thoughtful, still tugging at her hair as she stares into the ferns across from them.

"Yeah, I guess. I've never called It myself, but I guess my dad did all the time, judging by...all of this. The one time I did see It wasn't exactly fun. I told you, right?"

"Kinda? I mean, you said It was scary. Said Its voice was like a howling nightmare, or something equally dramatic. But I mean, there must be something we can do. Maybe we can... I don't know. How did you and your dad even find out about this Thing?"

Mariam shakes her head. "Someone from my dad's firm gave him a book before mom was diagnosed with cancer again. It's a huge leather thing with legit buckles and yeah. Like, it looks medieval or something, older than that even, but like, in mint condition? I don't know really how to describe it. But my dad got drunk after mom died, and he followed the directions, and voila! Ready-made monster in the study."

"Where would anyone find a book like that? And why would they give it to him?"

"Mom was a book collector. I think it was her 25th or something and some rich client? I don't know. I can't really remember. What's it matter, anyways?"

Camila's thoughtful look is back. "Maybe there's a reason. Maybe there's something in the book we can find to help us."

"Yeaaaahhhh... no." Mariam shakes her head and lets out a bark of laughter tinged with hysteria.

"Mariam, I don't want to live in this forest forever. I miss coffee. I miss showers. I miss being indoors. Please, we've got to try. Please."

"Where would we even start?"

"Mariam. Your house. Stop being stupid."

"Oh, God. I don't even know if it's still stable. I don't even know—"

But Camila's already jumped to her feet and is holding out her hand toward Mariam with an annoyingly enthusiastic smile.

"There's only one way to find out, isn't there?"

EVEN WITHOUT THE kids to slow them down, it takes four days of walking west before they find what was once a highway that they recognize. Mariam is almost certain it's the La Brea stretch of the 10, just collapsed and twisted on its pylons. It's too unstable to walk on, but they pick their way alongside its remains and keep heading west, toward the sea, toward home. At one time Mariam would have been able to drive this route with her eyes closed, but the city is all but unrecognizable, and she has to rely on fortuitous finds of buried street signs to point her way to the proper exit.

The jungle plays its usual tricks—tripping them up, sending flocks of giant, whirring dragonflies swarming into their path—but its fury seems dampened, somehow. Mariam hopes it's grown tired of trying to kill them. She can't help but worry about the others, left alone to fend for themselves against the forest, but if she's right about this, it won't really be interested in them anymore.

At the coast, they turn north, peering through the screen of angry, writhing vines at the ocean beyond, but there's no sign of the rescue teams Mariam had seen on her first journey here. Another day, two days, and they've reached what Mariam is fairly certain is her neighborhood. The forest has sunk into gloom, the dim sunlight fading quickly. Occasionally they pass a hulking, overgrown ruin, the original structure nearly impossible to make out amongst the trees growing up straight through it. Mariam counts: three, four, five houses from the corner. Home.

Like the others, her house is overrun with vines, moss, and every other conceivable kind of vegetation. A bloom of deep purple mushrooms the size of refrigerators has taken over the gable that used to house her bedroom window, and the roof is fuzzy with moss. Still, it's mostly standing. They linger by the mailbox for a moment, and Camila gives a low whisper, though her voice is finally regaining its strength. "You must've been loaded. Jesus Christ, Mariam. Pacific freaking Palisades?"

Mariam shrugs. "Yeah, I mean. Daddy was a partner in a big firm."

Camila gives her the side-eye. "I never would have guessed."

Not for the first time, Mariam wonders at Camila's background. "What about your parents?"

Camila shrugs. "They were immigrants. Mama worked at a hotel cleaning, and Papi worked in construction. That's how he knew Ishmael and how I got the babysitting job for the others. Anyway, should we go in?" Camila points her chin to the front door and Mariam nods.

"We can get in through the back. I know where the key should be."

Luckily the back door is intact, and Mariam successfully feels for the spare key under the flowerpot that is also, miraculously, still in place. The door swings open easily as if the hinges haven't been rusting in the oppressive humidity, as if the frame hasn't been rotting and infested with lichens. Inside, Mariam doesn't know what she expected, but it wasn't this: the house is practically spotless. Sure, there are a few vines here and there, but compared to other houses they've been to, Mariam's is pristine.

"Wow." Camila's fingers linger on a family portrait in the hall. "You were a cute baby. Is this...is she your mom?"

"Yeah."

"You look more like your dad, but you have her smile."

Mariam swallows back the lump in her throat. "No one's ever told me that before."

They make their way down the hallway toward her dad's study. That's where the book will be. As they get closer, Mariam can feel her shoulders relaxing. This is home, and the farther they go into the house, the more she can feel the jungle disappearing behind her. Even vines are fewer here, just a spidery network of little tendrils creeping along the wall. The smell is different too, not like the damp, vegetable odor that's been in her nose for a month now, but like home, like the incense her dad used to burn, with something else underneath. A sweet, sickly smell. Rot.

Three paces from the heavy study doors, the last of the vines stop. Mariam hesitates, glances at Camila, and then puts her hand on the doorknob. It's warm, and with a little pressure, the door to the study pushes open easily, and Mariam steps inside. Instantly, the last sounds of the forest disappear. It's silent but for their quiet breathing. There's not one sign of vegetation except the potted fern sitting by the window, the window that is suspiciously free of mildew spots or water stains.

Mariam takes another step into the study and reaches for Camila's hand without thinking. She wants to say something, but the stillness of the air makes talking seem like sacrilege.

The book should be in its usual place, laying open on a stand built into the bookshelves that line the wall to their left. There's the stand, and the rows of books, but where is the book? Mariam steps over to it, tugging Camila behind her.

The oversized tome is nowhere to be seen but lying in its place on the stand is a slim, black ledger, the soft leather cover unmarked by any title.

Mariam frowns before picking it up. It's heavier than it should be, and warm, and it's giving her the creeps, but it's not the right book.

"Is that it? I thought you said it looked medieval or something." Camila is the first to break the silence.

"I don't know."

"What do you mean?"

Mariam ignores Camila for a moment before opening the book to a random page.

...the following procedures dictate proper conduct for summoning the Steward and Associate, respectively, in conditions matching...

Mariam scans the page and suddenly drops the book. It thumps on the ground and Camila rushes to retrieve it from its undignified spot on the floor.

"What's wrong?"

"I think... I think you're right; this is it. I think the book changed. I think... I think when my dad became the new steward...read this."

Mariam jabs her finger at the page as Camila holds it up. "See, what else could this be? Nobody uses the word 'summon.'"

"Um...this is so freaking dense. Like, the language is so hard to read." Camila's face is doing that cute thing where she screws up her eyes. "I think you're right though. Which means your dad is the Steward, but what's this other ritual for? Associate. That's so weird. Maybe there's a glossary or something? I want to know what associate means."

Mariam leans against one of the wooden bookshelves. "Glossary?"

"Yeah... I want to study law, and this kinda reads like a weird law document. They usually define their terms at the beginning."

"Okay..." Mariam's eye wanders as Camila flips to the start of the book, and her eyes wander to the wall, where more pictures of her, mostly with Ammu. There's a picture of her learning the electric guitar under her uncle's dedicated tutelage, and Mariam wonders if her guitar is still here somewhere. Probably in the basement. In fact—

"Mariam?"

"What?" Mariam snaps out of her reverie at the sound of Camila's panicked tone. "What's wrong?"

"I think it's you...you're the associate." There's a tremor of horror in Camila's voice, tinged with fascination.

"What?"

Camila thrusts the book into her hands, and there, in italicized print, Mariam reads:

Associate: The party appointed by the Steward to receive certain benefits pertaining to the Steward's transformation. In the event that the Steward is unable to assume his responsibilities, becomes incapacitated, or is temporarily deemed unfit, the Associate will assume responsibility for the proper governance of all realms in question (see section 1.43.2) and must fulfill all contractual obligations signed into agreement by the Steward until such time as the Steward returns or a new Steward is chosen.

As described in section 1.1.2, the human Mariam Aboul-Nour took on the role of Associate to Steward Malik Aboul-Nour. See section 1.1.4 for lineage, attributes, and...

Mariam can't make herself read anymore. "What..."

"It said your name. It said you'll be held responsible." Camila tries to still her shaking hands, but Mariam can see she's freaked out. Hell, Mariam herself is freaked out. She never agreed to any of this!

But maybe she didn't have to. Maybe when she shook the Beast's hand, that was all It needed. Mariam doesn't really know how this has happened, but she can feel the anger building in her chest. She stifles it. It won't do them any good for her to throw a tantrum. She needs to focus.

They take advantage of the fading light to comb the book for instructions on how to summon the Beast, taking turns sitting on the desk with the slim volume on their knees and paging through the thin leaves. The text is dense, but strangely modern—recognizable—and Mariam can't help but see her father's personality in it. It's his book, without a doubt, the same way that monstrosity of a tome just seemed right for the monstrosity that appeared here all those years ago.

While Camila reads, Mariam moves slowly around the room, examining her father's possessions. On a whim, she flips the light switch and nearly screams when the lamps actually flicker on. There's definitely something weird going on with the house, but for now, she isn't complaining, as the light gives them more time to read. And besides, as Camila said, she's missed being indoors.

It's been hours, and Mariam is thinking of saying they should stop for the evening when Camila, triumphant, exclaims, "I found it!"

Mariam hurries over from the other side of the room, where she had been absentmindedly looking through her father's collection of stamps.

"I think this is it," Camila says again. "It has a list of previous stewards, see? And this is the most recent one. Alberich, son of Donar. So that must be Him, right?"

For some reason, Mariam had never even considered that It might have a name. But It must have had one once, when It was a human just like her dad, maybe just too curious about a book he had found. It was even a child once. Someone like little Hana or Carlos, with loving parents—or not. The idea that It was once human worries her. How could that thing ever have been a person? What is going to happen to her dad? To her?

Camila isn't preoccupied with the idea, though. She's already flipping to the appropriate page (section 56.3.2) where the book promises to detail the summoning ritual for Steward Alberich, son of Donar.

She got it right, Mariam thinks, chewing on her lip. Vegetation (flowers or fruit, in season), something of personal importance or great cost to the summoner, and a chant. It's all there, just like her father taught her. She didn't understand the words then and she doesn't understand them now, but now that she knows Its name, she wonders if it's Anglo-Saxon or something. Maybe It's even older. Who knows? Certainly not Mariam.

"So that's it," Camila says after they've had a chance to read it over. "What do we do now?"

"Sleep," Mariam says, and grabs the book from Camila to snap it shut. "I'm tired, and I'm not summoning a Demon, or whatever Mr. Alberich is now, in the middle of the night."

They decide to settle down in the living room, where they find familiar blankets, dry and intact as if the world outside hasn't grown over with hell-plants.

As they settle into the bed they've made of couch cushions, Mariam listens for the jungle night sounds that she's gotten used to, but it's nearly silent in the house. Eerie, to know that on the other side of the window is a forest full of the usual clicks and chirp and slithering things. Inside, it's almost like it never happened.

They've left the hall light on, and in its faint glow, Mariam can see the outline of Camila's face. Her eyes are wide open.

"What do you think the others are doing?" Camila eventually asks softly.

"I don't know," Mariam says. "Camila, you can...you can go back if you want. To be with them. You don't have to do this."

A moment later Camila's hand slips into hers under the blanket and gives it an almost aggressive squeeze. "Don't be ridiculous, Mariam. I came after you for a reason, okay?"

"Why?" Mariam asks. "Why did you come find me?"

Camila pulls her head closer and kisses her. "You know why." Then she rests her head on Mariam's chest and dozes off to sleep.

Chapter Fifteen

THERE'S TOO MUCH to do in the morning. They go outside and gather some of those mushrooms underneath her bedroom window—the small ones, not the giant ones—and Mariam finds her guitar in the basement. Part of her is screaming that she can't possibly think of sacrificing the guitar Ammu gave her before he left, but then...she can't find anything important to her in the house. She was never much at home anyway, with friends and acquaintances from another lifetime. Her room was just the place where she slept sometimes, and the sentimental stuff mostly belonged to her dad, not to her; the point of this exercise is to get the Beast to actually come this time. The guitar is definitely sentimental, and more importantly, she thinks it will work.

They go to her father's pristine study, close the door behind them, and assemble all their pieces. The plan, inasmuch as they have one, is this: summon the Beast, somehow convince It not to kill them in the first minute, persuade It that they should work together, and maybe devise a trap for her dad. Camila's been doing more reading, and from what she can understand, it seems that the power of the Stewards is actually quite limited. At least, they're bound by so many different rules and regulations that there must be a way to get Malik to do what they want.

When the time for the actual summoning comes, Mariam has tons of second-thoughts. About her guitar, about what they're actually going to say if it works, how Camila will react to the Creature...so many what-ifs, and not enough time to think them through.

Camila gets the book, and Mariam places her red guitar up next to the mushrooms. It looks super weird, and Mariam isn't sure she's ready when Camila gives her the book.

She feels sluggish, like she's in a half-remembered nightmare, and the unfamiliar words are foreign to her tongue. Not English or Arabic or even Russian. The phonemes are weird in her mouth, and Mariam all but stumbles through the ancient language.

Nothing happens for a moment, two moments, three. Mariam almost releases the breath she's holding, half in disappointment, half in relief. Then the ground begins to shake. A paperweight rolls off of her father's desk and thuds dully on the carpeted floor. In front of them, the mushrooms begin to sag and discolor. A mist seeps into the room from where the mushrooms sit, rippling over their damp skin like a living thing. The hairs on her arms and the back of her neck stand on end like the temperature has dropped, except it hasn't. Then—

Twang!

The strings of Mariam's guitar snap—twang! twang!—and Camila is suddenly clinging to Mariam's arm with a vice-like grip, her fingernails digging into Mariam's elbow.

Then there's half an instant when all the sound goes out of the world, and Mariam realizes the Beast is standing in front of them, though she can't remember when It got there. It's just as she remembers It from when she was a kid, the unholy monster in all its rotting glory, Its mask of fused human skulls sitting atop its head, Its fleshless hands raised by Its sides.

Who calls me?

There's that voice, the voice that nightmares are made of, the voice that sounds like a choir of haunted souls filling up her head. Mariam drops to her knees and clamps her hands over her ears to shut it out, but the sound worms its way through her fingers and shivers through her skull to fondle her brain.

I will not ask again. Its voice rings through the study, and Mariam feels her insides freeze. Part of her wants to shrink into the ground, and the other part of her wants to comfort Camila, who has dropped to the floor next to her, burying her face in Mariam's shoulder.

"It's me," Mariam says, her gaze fixed on the carpet in front of her.

Suddenly It's rising, towering over them in a surging mass of gristle and bone. Its joints click and pop and remind her of the unnatural snap in her father's shrug. She shrinks and forgets to breathe. The smell of rot intensifies, the low light of the study dims, and Mariam wants to disappear.

Ah. The Associate. Somehow, though It isn't actually speaking, Mariam detects the condescension dripping from Its words. *Why have you called me? Is not your Steward causing enough grief to my worlds?*

But Mariam doesn't have an answer—any answers at all. Under the Beast's fleshless glare, in the waft of rot and death that washes over them, her mind has gone blank.

"We want to help you, Alberich. We want to help you get Malik to take up the role of Steward."

Both Mariam and the Beast turn to look at Camila, who, though still crouching on the ground, returns the Monster's gaze calmly. Mariam can feel Camila's quick, shallow breathing next to her, and the moment that it stops when the Beast shifts, slowly, slowly, to settle Its horrific head just inches from Camila's face.

No one has called me by that name for a very long time. Its hand reaches out for Camila's cheek. Mariam grabs Camila's arm and jerks her back.

"Don't touch her!"

The Creature recoils and Mariam can swear It's blinking somewhere, the view obscured by Its hanging skin and mask. It's more a feeling than a visual, one of disorientation, as if the Beast is projecting Its thoughts and feelings into the room.

To Mariam's surprise, Camila clears her throat and stands, her knees not even shaking. "Mariam, it's fine. We just need to talk."

I am listening.

"Mariam had nothing to do with this," Camila says. Her voice doesn't tremble; it's just quiet and strong. She continues, "We've read the book. We want to get Malik to take up your mantle. We ...we don't know how. The book doesn't say, and we were hoping you knew of some way."

The Beast is silent for a moment. Its massive body shivers and clicks. *You, his Viceroy—his "Associate," as he has called you—wish to betray him? To bind him where he refuses to be bound?*

When It puts it like that, it sounds pretty awful, but Mariam swallows and nods. "Yes."

Malik's refusal to take responsibility for his domain is unprecedented. He should be learning at my side, an apprenticeship. There is much to learn for a human. If he fails to do so, this chaos will endure. Even I cannot halt the things he has set into motion. He must be brought to heel. The Beast turns again to Mariam, fixing her with what she could swear is a leering grin. *Or his viceroy could take up the mantle in his stead.*

"Not an option," says Camila. "She never agreed to this. He did."

The Beast continues its attentions on Mariam, ignoring Camila now. There's something like laughter in her ears. *If you will not take his place, there is only one path that I can see. The book in ages past contained the binding spells, but that knowledge has long since been lost. Not since before my time, before my predecessor's time has anyone known of them. But with my help...perhaps you might construe one yourself.*

"What?" Mariam clears her throat and continues. "But how will I know what will bind him?"

Spells of this kind require virgin blood and the blood of kin. Both of you can contribute.

Camila blushes and squeaks, "I'm not...I'm not a virgin."

The ancient laws care little for human convulsions and excretions. You have never performed magic. Your blood is pure.

"Oh." Camila's nose has scrunched up.

Mariam's fear loosens. The feeling goes back in her legs and she finally manages to stand.

"And what else? That's not much to go on."

The Beast rumbles from deep within itself. *The knowledge is lost, but the trappings of magic are only ways to channel desire. You are his viceroy. Only you, I suspect, will be able to bind him, if you so desire it. Find the things that would call to him, that would keep him, and speak your power over him in their midst.*

"Speak what?"

Whatever is necessary. You must decide. I will help you to hold him when the times comes. Even now his strength is too great for a human to manage. Use this to call me when you are ready. The smell of rotting vegetation disappears, and in its place lies a little bit of bone carved into a skull.

Camila collapses into a chair and shudders.

"Okay, you were right, that Thing is super creepy." Camila rubs her hands together as if she's cold, and Mariam nods.

Chapter Sixteen

THEY STAY IN the house for a few days, but both, by unspoken agreement, avoid the study, having shut the doors firmly behind them after the whole Beast incident. The bedrooms are intact, but for some reason, Mariam can't stomach having Camila either in her childhood bedroom or her dad's, so they set up camp in the living room, where the couch cushions make for a decent mattress. In the mornings, they strategize in the kitchen over bowls of oatmeal—an unimaginable luxury courtesy of the unlooted pantry.

Mariam has decided they need to go to her father's office and take her mother's ashes, but beyond that, she feels stuck. They'll need words, won't they? Maybe Russian for her mom? But then, dad never did learn Russian. Or Arabic? He grew up speaking Arabic, but it was Ammu who taught Mariam the little bit she knows, and she isn't sure her grammar is good enough for her to actually come up with a meaningful spell. In the end, it's Camila who reminds her that her father's book is written in English, and that settles it.

While rummaging in her father's bedroom, which feels so weird, she finds her mother's wedding rings in an old jewelry box by the bed. She hasn't seen them in years, and she sits on her dad's bed for a moment, willing the tears away. It's so hard. It's so hard and so unfair, and Mariam can feel the tension in her shoulders solidify. She wants to wallow just a little bit, but she knows that Camila is in the kitchen downstairs, heating up some soup on the working stove.

The bit of bone she keeps in her pocket is ever-warm, and not just it's-LA-so-it's-always-hot-warm, but more like it's alive, radiating its own heat. She puts the rings in the same pocket and meanders downstairs to the kitchen.

"Hi." Camila greets her with a kiss, and Mariam smiles despite herself. One day, when this is all over, she imagines a world where she and Camila work together to make a home. Sentimental stuff, she knows, but she can't help it when Camila is so affectionate. It makes her hopeful for a future that may never be hers.

They break the kiss. "Hi," Mariam says dopily.

Before she can continue, Camila takes the soup off the burner and says, "I had an idea. The words you want to use. Did your parents ever sing you lullabies or did they have a song or something? There's power in music and sentimentality, and maybe... I don't know. It's a thought."

Mariam bites her lip, thinking. Her dad was never the lullaby type. Did her parents have a song? She shrugs. "Don't worry about it. I'll figure it out."

"We're going tomorrow." Camila waves a wooden spoon between them. "Figure it out soon."

Mariam nods. "I know, I know, I'm working on it." She dips her head to whisper conspiratorially, "Besides, I'm magic with words, babe."

Camila bursts into laughter and begins to pour the soup out into bowls. "You'd better be."

AS WEIRD AS it is to be living in the ghost of her old neighborhood, Mariam would have happily stayed there with Camila as long as the jungle let them. It's easy to forget the murder-forest outside when they've got food and light and each other on the inside. But eventually the next day comes, marked with soft filtered sunlight on Camila's sleeping face, and there's very little Mariam can do to stop the passage of time. Mariam leans over and kisses the tip of Camila's nose to wake her.

"Hey, sleepy. Today's the day. Time to go catch a demon. Want some oatmeal?"

Camila's face scrunches up for a moment, but then she sighs, and reaches up to pat Mariam's cheek. "Yeah. I'll go heat it up. You make sure everything's ready, okay?"

SHE'S TRYING TO exude confidence for Camila's sake, but Mariam's stomach is rioting against her, reminding her that she still hasn't figured out the right words. When Camila asks her, she smiles as cavalier as she can manage and says, "Yeah, I figured it out last night."

Why she lies, she has no idea, but the relief on Camila's face is difficult for her to bear under the weight of her lie.

When they leave her childhood home, Mariam feels a sense of heaviness drop onto her shoulders and has to fight the urge to turn around. The only reason she's going through with this, she realizes, is because she doesn't want Camila to think she's a coward. Camila, despite no invulnerability, is braver than anyone Mariam has ever met, and she wants to live up to that. She wants to be brave, even when her heart is hammering in her chest.

"You okay?"

Mariam flashes her teeth in what she hopes looks like a smile. "Never better."

"You're allowed to be nervous. I am. And like, he's not even my dad."

Mariam's false grin falters. "Yeah, I'm a bit freaked out, but you know. Greater good and hot showers and not-canned food and all that jazz."

Camila giggles, a rush of pink coloring her cheeks. "You're so funny."

Mariam doesn't feel particularly comedic. She feels sick.

The jungle doesn't give her time to dwell on it, though. The creeping vines and stinging insects are almost a relief from her thoughts, and she tries to focus on stomping through the living foliage instead of imagining what will happen when she either can't get her dad to come, or when she does. She's not sure which eventuality she's more nervous about.

As usual, the streets have been overgrown almost beyond recognition, but Mariam knows this area well and successfully guides them past a series of barely noticeable landmarks toward the cluster of taller ruins where her dad worked. They make it to the remnants of her father's office in Brentwood in the late afternoon, having taken only a couple short breaks for water in between. Mariam's calves ache from all the walking, and she takes a moment to stretch before they set to prying open what used to be the building's automatic doors. It takes them a good while, but eventually, when they're both panting with the exertion, they give way with a god-awful screech, and the girls slip inside.

The lobby is almost as Mariam remembers, except that the slick tile has been carpeted over with moss, and there are vine hanging in loops and straggly strings from the ceiling, and that the fountain in the middle is gone— replaced by a tree that's growing straight up through the high ceiling and into the floors above.

"Wow, fancy," Camila says. "What did your dad do again?"

"He was an entertainment lawyer. Worked with copyright and stuff. Boring, boring, boring, but he liked it, so I guess that's what matters."

Of course, the elevator doesn't work, and of course, Daddy worked on the eighth floor. They're both huffing and puffing, and Mariam has to count the flights of stairs to ensure they're on the right floor in the dark stairwell. She miscounts, and they stumble on to the floor above her dad's before finally getting to the right place.

This high above the ground, the office is less affected by the jungle below, though the tree from the lobby has broken through here too, on its way up to the sky a few floors up. Clusters of ferns wave gently in the breeze from the broken windows. It's oddly peaceful.

"So which one is his?" Camila asks, and Mariam gestures to a door on her left.

They share a brief glance, then push in the door together. The hinges have rusted, and the door groans in complaint before giving way and sending them both stumbling into the room.

It's nothing special—Malik was never one for too many personal effects in his work life. The books that line the walls give off the slightly sweet scent of rotting paper, but it's so much better than the stink of fungus down below that neither of them mind.

Now that they're here, there doesn't seem much point in talking, so they begin their preparations, setting up a circle in the room, using the desk as the pedestal where they'll put her mom's rings. It doesn't take long, though Mariam delays as much as she can, adjusting and re-adjusting the placement of just about everything they've brought.

Finally, Camila catches her eye. "You ready?" she asks.

Mariam is sweating, and it's not just from the stairs. She's been trying to think of the right words all day, and once they summon Alberich, she'll have to have the words prepared.

She doesn't hesitate, though, just nods determinedly and passes the bone-carving to Camila. They've brought a knife with them as well, for the kin-blood and the virgin-blood.

"As ready as I'll ever be."

They set the bone-skull in the middle of the table and in a moment, the Beast's presence fills the once elegant office. It fills an entire corner of the room, hunching to fit beneath the low ceiling, and blocks out most of the light from the windows.

It says nothing, just looks at Mariam and undulates unnervingly beneath the tatters of Its skin. She has the awful feeling that It knows she isn't prepared, and they stand in silence until Camila nudges her.

Mariam breathes. Then she breathes again and reaches into her pocket to pull out the rings. Just one more moment's hesitation, then she places them in the center of the desk.

"Camila?" But Camila is already there, her hand held out and her gaze unflinching.

Mariam makes a quick slice into Camila's palm, then holds the hand steady over the rings until a few thick drops of blood fall over them. The rings sizzle as the liquid touches them.

Mariam drops Camila's wrist, steps to the edge of the circle, clears her voice, puts as much intent as she possibly can into her words, and calls, "Malik Fatin Aboul-Nour, I summon you here by the power of virgin blood. Steward, your associate seeks your presence. Here, in the place of your life work, with these, the symbols of your love. Come now and answer our summons." She knows as she says them, how ridiculous the words sound, like cheesy lines from one of the terrible movies her father's clients made. Camila's eyes are wide with anticipation, the Beast's face impossible to read. They wait for the space of three heartbeats...four...five. Nothing happens. No wind, no smells, nothing. So maybe a different tactic.

"Daddy, uh... it's me, it's Mariam, and I need your help."

Then the air does shift, and Mariam realizes that's probably all she ever needed to say. She needs his help. Suddenly, she feels sick again, and this time she knows what it is. It's guilt.

He materializes in the middle of the circle, crouched on his hands and knees in his flawless suit. He gasps, sucking in a breath of the air that suddenly tastes like ozone. Something horrible shifts in Mariam's chest as she watches him. This is wrong, she realizes. He looks vulnerable. He looks human. His eyes circle the room, first alighting on Mariam, Camila, and then, inevitably, on the Beast.

"Mariam, what is this?"

"Sorry, Daddy. I have to. I'm sorry, but I have to." Tears blur her vision, but even she can see her dad look to the window and begin the lunge to make his escape.

Camila cries out, but before she can reach for him, vines come writhing from the ceiling, wrapping around Malik's chest and binding him to the table. The Beast surges forward to stand over Malik and direct further vines to grab at Malik's ankles.

Mariam sets her teeth, wiping the tears from her eyes. She makes a deep cut on her palm with the knife, slicing deep so that she can get blood out before it heals.

In the brief moment before she can touch him with the blood, she makes the mistake of looking her father in the eye.

"Mariam, please, don't do this to me."

She considers, for half a second, not doing it to him, and as she does, he shifts, shivers, and grabs Camila, twisting her arms behind her back and reaching up to hold her by the throat.

"I'll take her with me. I will kill her," he hisses. "I will kill her, and it will not be a merciful death, Mariam."

Camila struggles against his hand. "Do it, Mariam! Do it for everyone! Don't worry about me."

The Beast's voice grates against Mariam's ears. *It must be done now, Viceroy. I cannot hold him long. Forget the girl, we do not need her blood.*

It's right: Malik is shuddering now, twisting out of the Beast's vines, wrenching Camila this way and that as his body flickers in and out of form.

It would be easy: all she needs to do is reach out her bleeding hand to touch him and bind him with her blood, and he would be bound. But—Mariam drops her knife, looks at the Beast and shakes her head.

"I can't. I can't let him hurt Camila." And that's true, but it's not the whole truth.

The Beast regards her for a moment, but Malik is breaking through the last of his vines. In a blink, the Beast is gone, and Malik shudders one more time, turning inward into himself, disappearing just the same.

Camila thuds to the floor, and Mariam rushes to her. "I'm sorry. I'm sorry. I couldn't. I'm sorry."

She's not sure which she's apologizing for—for saving her girlfriend or for failing to kill her, but it's all she can think to say.

Fourth Interlude

LUCI SQUINTS OUT at the forest beyond the cave. Nothing moves, and today the air's still enough that even the little fluttery leaves up top are quiet. It's been very, very quiet since Mariam and Camila disappeared. No one knows what's happened to them, not even Eun-Ji. Eun-Ji doesn't even want to talk about it, and Luci doesn't know what to do. What's she supposed to do anyway? She's barely a teenager. She keeps watch during the day, just in case Mariam and Camila decide to come back.

She doesn't think they will because, in Luci's experience, people don't come back. They just go away, and you never hear from them ever again. That's what happened with Mamae and Daddy, that's what happened with Bob and Dave, and yeah, so dying wasn't Nayara's fault—and maybe it wasn't Bob and Dave's either—but they're all gone.

To be perfectly honest, Luci didn't really have strong feelings about Mariam either way, but she really looked up to Camila. Luci feels the same vague sense of betrayal she felt when she was taken from her parents. Betrayal and thinly veiled anger. Luci is very angry, all the time. Bob once told her she had every right to be angry, what with her parents being put in prison, and of course, as he liked to remind her, all the changes happening to her body like hormones making her emotions go up and down. Bob was so nice. He was so nice. So was Camila. She guesses some people just aren't meant to stay in your life forever.

Hana's been asking after them, but Eun-Ji doesn't have answers and neither does Luci. Why would they leave? It's not fair.

Luci huffs and folds her arms across her chest. People suck. They suck big time.

Behind her, she can hear Eun-Ji digging through the packs for food. They're running low, just a few cans of tuna and several varieties of beans left, so Ishmael left this morning to make a grocery run. It's safer now than before, at least that's what Ishmael says. The forest's anger seems to have disappeared along with Mariam.

Tink tink.

Luci leaps up, thinking it's Ishmael back with some more food. She scans the tree line at the edge of the clearing, but it's just as still as before.

Tink tink.

Luci frowns, stepping out of the overpass's shadow, but before she even gets to the fire, she feels a tug on her shirt, and suddenly she's being jerked to the side. A hand clamps itself over her mouth; another holds her wrists behind her back. Luci blinks, trying to get her bearings. A group of five or six gaunt men surround her, the first people other than her family she's seen in months. Their faces are pale underneath but smeared with jungle grime where they aren't obscured by greasy bandanas and scraggly beards. Something hard and sharp presses against her ribs.

"Don't scream," someone says into her ear.

She can feel her panic rising, can feel her heartbeat stutter erratically, but she tries to keep calm. Luci's a black Latina, and even if this isn't really America anymore, she knows what white men can be capable of. She doesn't want to give them any excuse to hurt her, though if they are planning on doing that anyways, screaming or not screaming isn't going to matter.

Someone, maybe their leader, a man with light brown hair and a copper beard, nods and the one holding her jostles her toward the entrance of the cave. She hears a metallic click, and Luci's extensive movie-watching experience tells her it's a gun.

The entire group moves now, and then she's staring down the barrel of the aforementioned gun. She can't even cry.

They step into the entrance of the cave, holding her out front. Though their bodies block most of the light, Luci can see Eun-Ji freeze, her eyes going wide. Eun-Ji stands slowly from her place on the floor. Where are Hana and Carlos? Luci squints into the back of the cave, hoping they're hidden, hoping they have the sense to stay still and stay quiet. They're just babies.

"What do you want?" Eun-Ji asks, her voice steady and clear. One of the men sneers, but copper-beard holds his hand out.

"We want food and supplies. Blankets, the canned stuff, and especially—" He points to the stash of lighters Ishmael keeps in his corner of the cave. "—those lighters. You are going to get everything and roll it up in a blanket for me and my men to take. And you're going to do it now, or this one gets her head blown off."

Eun-Ji stands still for just half a second before copper-beard barks, "Now!"

She jumps, but hurries to obey, glancing over her shoulders every few moments at the men. Luci tries to give Eun-Ji a reassuring nod, but she's pretty sure her face is more of a frozen grimace than anything else.

Luci can't gauge the time that passes. Part of her hopes Ishmael comes to save them, though she doesn't like his chances against six guys with guns. Hundreds of scenarios play out in her head, and each one ends with everyone dead. She tries to stop thinking through the clanking of tins and muffled thumps as the supplies are dropped on a pile of blankets.

Finally, Eun-Ji inches forward with a bulky bundle in her arms. Luci can see how her knuckles have gone white where she's gripping the blanket. Eun-Ji holds it out towards copper-beard, and he nods for one of the other men to take it from her.

"That wasn't so hard, now was it?" His voice is quiet, but Luci can almost hear the mocking smile in it. Eun-Ji steps back, holding shaking hands down by her sides.

"You can leave us alone. We won't cause you any trouble," she says.

A few of the men behind Luci laugh. Copper-beard steps forward to stand in front of Eun-Ji.

"I'm thinking about it. Where are the kids?"

Eun-Ji's eyes snap up. Luci can see her trying to contain her fear, mask it with anger.

"They're not here," she lies. "They went with my husband."

"No," Copper-beard says quietly, stepping closer to Eun-Ji. "We saw him go. Alone. Where are they?"

The guy holding Luci tightens his grip to the point of pain. Luci can't help but cry out.

That seems to be it for Carlos. He charges out from the shadows, his fists balled up and rage distorting his dear little face.

"Leave Luci alone!" Eun-Ji tries to grab him but he slips away too fast for her reaching arms, hurtling toward the men.

Copper-beard laughs and plucks Carlos into the air by his collar, nodding to Eun-Ji. "I'm guessing the little one is hiding away in the back like this one was. Don't lie to me again, woman," he says over Carlos's fearless struggles.

He hefts the writhing Carlos in front of him, holding him by the shoulders.

Carlos, dear little Carlos, spits into his face.

Copper-beard regards the boy a moment, letting the spittle drip down his cheek. Carlos quiets for the first time under his stare.

"Listen, boy. You try something like that again—any of you disrespect me like that again—and I will kill you. I will kill you and your momma and your sisters—whatever you all are. Every single one of you. Don't you spit in my face again, understand?"

Carlos looks back to where Hana is hiding, and for the first time, he looks scared.

"Apologize," Copper-beard demands.

"Sorry," Carlos, bless him, his voice comes out strong and not even a little bit sarcastic. Copper-beard puts Carlos down but keeps his large bony hand on Carlos's tiny shoulder.

"Anyone else have anything to say?"

Silence.

He nods then, and the gun moves from Luci's face to the back of her head. They push her forward and she stumbles, her legs numb with terror, toward Eun-Ji who catches her.

Then copper-beard lets Carlos go, and all the men leave, silent but for the tink tink of a gun bouncing against someone's leg.

Only then does Luci allow herself to cry.

Later, when Ishmael comes back with his backpack full of much-needed food, he finds them huddled in the back of the cave, clinging together while Hana sniffles. She hasn't let go of Luci since it got dark. Eun-Ji tells him what happened.

Ishmael hugs them all close, checks Luci for bruises, and kisses the top of Hana's head.

When they're all fed from the food he brought back and snuggled down in their blankets, he takes Eun-Ji outside.

Luci can't hear everything they say, but words drift in from outside, and she strains to understand Ishmael's gentle rumble, Eun-Ji's voice between sobs.

"Do you know what they could have done to you?"

"Of course I know, I—"

"I have to find them."

"You can't leave us now, not with—"

"We have to get them back, Eun-Ji, we can't have this happen again."

Ishmael comes back in only to grab his pack, then hurries back into the dark outside. He leaves them his shotgun, but it doesn't make Luci feel any safer at all.

Chapter Seventeen

WITH VERY LITTLE to keep them in her old home, Mariam and Camila have started trying to find their way back to the overpass. The jungle is no longer trying to attack them, even after her failed attempt at binding her dad, and maybe Eun-Ji will let her come back. Even if she doesn't, Mariam can live outside the cave. She can't be by herself, she's decided, and she can't be without Camila.

Camila had understood. She had even admitted her bravery was a sham. She was afraid, so afraid of dying, when it came down to it.

Though they don't know how to express it, the idea of getting back together with the others is appealing, too, for two teenage girls who just want some comfort after all this madness. They miss everyone. Ishmael and Luci and Carlos and Hana, even Eun-Ji. Mariam has found she misses the older woman's knowledge and steadiness.

They've found their way back to the river, and Mariam even thinks she recognizes this spot as one of their old camps before they found the overpass. At any rate, there are the damp remains of a campfire here, already fuzzed over with new moss, but recognizable.

Mariam is already hours into a fitful sleep when the snapping of vines and crackling of the plant life behind them jerks her awake. She scrabbles upright, holding out her hatchet and thinking that maybe it's one of those monkeys or any of the other unpleasant jungle surprises, or maybe even a person who wants their supplies. It could be any number of things.

"Easy, Mariam. It's me." Ishmael's deep voice calls out from the shadow between two trees. "I've been looking for you two for ages."

"Ishmael?" Camila's sleepy voice rises up from behind Mariam, and a rustling indicates that she's getting up.

Mariam drops the hatchet in surprise and her defenses fall away.

"Yeah, well."

They stand before each other, silent. The forest has gotten to Ishmael; in the light of the fire she can see he's all acid burns and it looks like he's stumbled a couple of times, but besides that and some scrapes, he seems okay. Mariam opens her mouth to say... she's not quite sure. She settles with, "We were coming back. You look like hell." Her voice comes out gruff. That would be the lump in her throat.

"I can take it." He smiles at her, white teeth bright in the light of her fire. "Besides. I had to find you."

He sighs and gestures to the floor next to her bed. "Can I join you?"

Mariam nods and settles back onto the ground with him. Camila rests her head on Mariam's lap.

"We need you, Mariam. And you too, Camila. We didn't realize how much until...some men came to camp a few days ago. I wasn't there. They—"

"Did they hurt anyone? What happened?" Mariam can't help but interrupt—her body's suddenly taut with fear. How could she have not realized this was a possibility? What if—?

"They're fine. Everyone's fine. They took food and some other supplies, but it could've...they could've...they could've done anything and..." Ishmael trails off, and Mariam suspects he's swallowing tears. When he speaks again his voice is unsteady, pleading. "I need you to help me protect them. I can't do it alone."

Mariam looks down at her hands to give Ishmael some privacy. Of course she wants to help them. Of course.

"Is Eun-Ji still mad at me?"

Ishmael shakes his head. "She's angry. She's hurt. Did you know she left her boyfriend when he started treating Hana badly? Appealed for sole custody when he started calling Hana names and hurting her. Eun-Ji will do anything for that kid. And usually she's right, but this time she was wrong. The forest is dangerous, but I don't trust the people who've survived this place."

Mariam shakes her head, then starts to laugh, almost hysterically. "I never told you, did I? My dad. He was killing people who got too close to us. I guess he stopped when I left. That's why we'd found all those bodies. I found out the day I told you about the summoning. I guess I just never thought to..." She can't finish the sentence, the horror of it too much. She needs her dad to protect these people. She needs her dad to ensure that no one hurts them. What if she's ruined things by trying to bind him and failing?

"Well, that would explain why nothing like this had happened yet. Though you probably should have told us that, too." He looks like he's gone past anger and just gotten to the other side exhausted.

"I know. There was just too much to say." She sighs. "I was coming back anyways. We tried...we tried to fix this, but I couldn't do what needed to be done."

"I'll ask you about it some other time. I want to get back as soon as we can."

"Okay. It's nearly morning, anyway. Do you want to rest?"

"No, I shouldn't even have left them for this long." Ishmael stands again, lifting his pack. "Anything could happen."

Mariam and Camila stand too. It doesn't take them long to pack up their things, so soon they're following Ishmael into the dark, heading back toward home.

THEY GET BACK in the early morning, and Luci is already up tending the fire. When she sees them, her hands go still, her mouth hangs slack for a moment, and then she turns back toward the embers, face creased with some kind of emotion.

"You left," Luci says. She's speaking more to Camila, Mariam thinks, but Mariam answers anyway.

"We had to. I'm sorry."

"That's so stupid. You didn't have to leave. No one has to leave, but you did, you—"

Ishmael interrupts. "We asked her to leave. Me and Eun-Ji. We thought...she told us she was the reason the jungle was worse, so we thought it'd be safer for us if she left."

Luci raises her eyebrows, unimpressed. "So what, you asked Camila to go too?"

Camila answers for herself this time. "I didn't want Mariam to be alone. I had to go with her."

Luci rolls her eyes. "Whatever. You're here now, I guess. Did Ishmael tell you about the jerks with the guns?"

Mariam nods, about to apologize, or something, but in that moment, Hana comes running out of the cave, shouting her head off at no one in particular, "I hear Mariam! Where is she?!" Carlos is not far behind, and stutters to a stop just in front of Camila before launching himself at her legs and nearly sobbing, "ImissedyouImissedyouI'msogladyoucameback." Luci sighs and finally joins the group hug that's forming, resting her head on Camila's shoulder.

Eun-Ji emerges from the underpass, too. She embraces Camila, then steps back and watches them all with a strange smile. Tear tracks mark her face and every so often she reaches down to pat Hana's head, but she won't even look at Mariam.

And maybe she's right, but maybe not. Maybe Mariam doesn't have to always pay for her father's mistakes.

Speaking of good-old-dad, he must have gotten over her trying to betray him and everything. After the sun has gone down, they hear a thump just outside the entrance of the cave. Something rolls into the collapsed overpass, and Ishmael goes to greet it. He stops it with his foot, examines it for a moment, and then calls Mariam, Camila, and Eun-Ji over.

"I'm guessing this is your dad's handiwork?" he asks. Mariam has to swallow down a wave of sick. It's a human head, its blank eyes and red beard glinting in the firelight. Something about the smell of the body, the rotting organic matter smell, makes Mariam think Ishmael's right.

It's a grotesque welcome-back gift, but from the head's copper beard and brown hair, Mariam surmises this is the leader of the group that attacked Luci and the others. Instead of disgust, Mariam feels relief and she shudders when she recognizes a twisted sense of giddiness welling up inside of her. She almost retches then and is relieved when Ishmael takes the severed-head and wraps it in a cloth.

"I'll get rid of this when it's light out."

The others just nod, and Ishmael tucks the cloth-wrapped head into a corner near the mouth of the cave.

MARIAM STICKS CLOSE to the camp for a few days after they return—she's missed them more than she let herself believe, and it feels like some kind of small betrayal to stray, even a little, from their side. But since the incident with the men, Ishmael has been too wary to leave the group for long, so they've been surviving on nearby fruits and a dwindling supply of canned beans. They need more to eat—the kids need protein—so she volunteers to make a trip to the abandoned grocery store if the way is still passable.

This morning, the air outside the cave is thick with a clinging mist that wraps itself around her wrists and ankles as she walks. Phantom sounds follow her through the trees, clicks and hisses and the shifting slither of plants that are too alive.

She stomps over ferns and bushes, not bothering to keep an eye out for danger. If her dad is so hellbent on protecting her, they might as well take advantage of it, right? But when she pauses for a moment and the sound of her own boots ceases, she realizes: the forest is too quiet. She can't remember when the small sounds in the trees stopped, but all the sudden there's that smell, rotting fruit, the one that haunts her memories and nightmares. The hairs on her arms and the back of her neck stand on end, and something feels off: this quiet, for one thing, and the way the mist ripples over her damp skin like a living thing, for another.

She gasps and stumbles as the mist coalesces into a familiar, hulking shape and the smell of death surrounds her. And then there's that voice, though it's more frightening than the last time she heard it. Less friendly, as if that were somehow possible. She supposes she should have expected this

Do not be afraid. I have not come to hurt you, child.

She doesn't look up, just concentrates on trying not to cry. She very much doubts It's not here to hurt her. She hates this thing. She hates It she hates It she hates It; why can't It just leave her alone?

If you cannot do what needs to be done, then we must do things my way.

Somehow, she finds her voice, and it's so small in her own ears, so small and quiet and alone. "I had no choice. I couldn't let Camila die."

And yet you reap all these benefits. My forest leaves you in peace, and still, you have your father's blessing. Its voice is suddenly more subdued, intimate, like Its putrid lips are at her ear, hissing their intent. *You made a deal, once, and you are still bound.* Its skeletal fingers hover over her downturned face, making a caressing motion close to her cheek. It doesn't touch her, but the proximity leaves her skin crawling. Mariam shudders.

No matter. Enough of the past. I am here to make you another offer. One you might find more appealing than the one your father made.

"I'm not interested in making any more deals with you."

Ah, but you see, you will be interested in this one. The creature pauses, and when It speaks again, Mariam can swear there are threads of glee woven through Its tapestry of voices. *It concerns your friends.*

Her head snaps up and she stands, raising her hatchet.

"I won't let you hurt them!"

It shudders, rises until It's blocking out what little sky she can see. The trees around them seem to curve in toward her, creaking and groaning with the strain of it. The Beast's bones are trembling and so are hers. She shrinks and forgets to breathe. *You will hear me,* It roars, and though Mariam can't be sure that It's actually making any sound, the voice fills her head with a deafening clamor. *I will accept no insolence from the likes of you.*

Mariam is sufficiently cowed. It settles back into a slightly less towering form.

I will give you one week. One week to say your goodbyes, whatever you must. Then I will return. You will agree to give up your life, and allow me to take you to the Realm of the Dead.

"Hell," she interrupts, because she's heard her father use those words before. "And why would I do that?"

It laughs, perhaps, if that grating crackle can be called a laugh. *In return, if all goes well, your friends will live comfortably. Your world restored to its...* It swivels Its horned head in disdain, *...less vegetal state.*

Understanding blooms like a cold light between her ears. "I didn't think it worked that way."

Not quite. You will die. Your father will make a deal to save your life, and in doing so will bind himself. It is a favorable exchange, for you. Think: the child, the small one. She could have a life worth living. Wouldn't you like that?

Mariam's mouth goes dry despite the fetid damp in the air. A life worth living. She could give it to them all.

"What if it doesn't work? What if he doesn't come for me?" Fear wraps itself around her spine. "I made him angry…"

The voice invades her thoughts to say, *Think on it. I will not make this offer twice, and if you do not agree, I will again release the forest against you, and against them. I will not be merciful.*

Suddenly Mariam is alone, left only with the stench of Its decay steeping in her lungs.

SHE TRUDGES TO the grocery store and back, her thoughts an agitated swarm of confusion. She isn't paying attention to where she's walking, but it's okay. The vines lie dormant, and occasionally even move out of her way in slow, respectful contractions. How convenient. How kind. She'd kick them for good measure, but her thoughts are elsewhere, laced with choral laughter and rot.

This is it. This is her chance to actually protect them for good. This is her chance to…to what exactly? Die? She would essentially be killing herself, just like her mom did all those years ago—blood on the carpet brains in her hair smell of gunpowder and death death dea—Mariam has to lean against a tree to retch before she can continue.

But isn't it the right thing to do? The lives of the many as opposed to the lives of the few and all of that, and what's one life compared to seven? To seven million, or however many families like hers are clawing their way through survival in this god-awful place? Besides, if it works, she won't die. Daddy will come rescue her, won't he? Didn't he do all this for her in the first place? Suddenly

Mariam isn't so sure as to her father's motives, and the uncertainty scares her more than she would ever have expected.

She doesn't cry. She feels number than anything else, conflicted and ill.

When she makes it back home with her pack of supplies, she greets them with false cheer in her voice. "Hey, everyone."

"Mariam's back!" Hana shouts, running to the edge of the circle of firelight, but no further. Despite the fact that the forest has left them alone for weeks now, she is still afraid of the entrance of the cave. Mariam comes in and scoops her up, throwing her in the air. It's good to hear Hana giggle, carefree like a little girl should be.

A life worth living.

Her stomach lurches, and she sets Hana down on the ground heavily. "What's wrong, Mariam?" Hana asks, her little hand taking Mariam's and tugging on it. "Did something bad happen?" she asks, and there's such genuine concern in her dear face that Mariam has to smile and squeeze her hand to reassure her.

"No," Mariam chokes on laughter and bile. "Everything's good, baby. Look, I brought some real food. And it's a beautiful day out." The taste in her mouth reminds her of the price of this peace.

AS FAR AS food hauls go, this one was pretty worthwhile. They break out two cans of mandarins to celebrate. Carlos and Hana go whooping around the fire in their enthusiasm for the sweet fruit.

Not, however, before Eun-Ji and Mariam have a moment alone. They're picking some of the passion fruit-apples to go along with dinner, when Eun-Ji says, with a quiet edge of steel in her voice, "It's been quiet since you've been gone. And quiet, now that you're back. Did you fix it?"

Mariam pretends not to hear. She doesn't want to talk about it right now, or ever if she can help it, but Eun-Ji pushes. "We deserve to know. It's our lives—my baby's life," she says, and Mariam tries not to look, but when she glances over, she sees the storm clouds gathering in Eun-Ji's eyes.

Mariam's chest pulls tight on itself. She's not ready to talk about what's happening, what's going to happen, but Eun-Ji's gaze is unrelenting.

The words tumble out of her mouth, one after another. "We tried to get my dad to take responsibility. It didn't work; Camila almost died, but I think—I think we convinced the forest it's not my fault. It's leaving us, all of us, alone. That's all I know."

It's not the whole truth, and Eun-Ji must know it, because she hesitates and opens her mouth like she's about to say something. Ultimately, Eun-Ji leaves with suspicion in her eyes, taking the fruit they've picked with her back to camp.

THEY SPEND THE evening outside, sitting in a circle backlit by the light from the fire at the cave's mouth. Luci passes around a few cans of garbanzo beans, and they eat without the walls of the cave pressing in around them. They talk. They laugh. Carlos does an impression of the vine-spider, and for the first time, it's funny instead of terrifying.

Mariam scoops up her beans in silence. Camila's sitting next to her, her shoulder pressing up against Mariam's, and she can feel the other girl shaking with laughter—real laughter—and humming her contentment. Camila's happy; they all are, with their constant mantle of fear lifted and the dark of the forest seeming just a little less oppressive now that the slitherings in the brush don't mean to kill. Now that Mariam's here with her hatchet, Ishmael sitting watch with his gun leaning against his knee. They feel safe, and it shows.

It can't last, though. It won't last, unless—unless— Mariam wobbles to her feet suddenly, feeling her gut churn as her thoughts turn to rotting fruit and rotting flesh. She leaves her plate on the ground and stumbles off into the trees, out of sight of the camp. She doesn't look back, but she doubts anyone's noticed because Carlos's still waving his arms about like the world's cutest vegetal hell-beast. It's pretty entertaining, she has to admit.

There's not that much to be afraid of out here, not for her anyway, ordinary dangers aside, and besides, there's her hatchet swinging at her hip. *You're welcome, sweetie.* She wants to throw it away. She wants to break it over her knee. She wants to grip it tight and cut down every tree in this goddamn forest because...what? Mariam sinks down and lets the damp seep into her knees. Her fingers dig into the moss and she cries.

Because she is afraid. All of this, and she's still just a scared little girl. She doesn't want to die. She doesn't want to die and that's the simple truth of it, but she doesn't want them to die either. Not Eun-Ji or Ishmael, not Luci or Carlos. Not Hana. Not Camila. Not a single one of them.

She's shaking, still, letting herself sob and gasp and cry salty tears, when she hears a rustle behind her, and then a voice—a little voice.

"Mariam?"

It's Hana. Of course it is, and Mariam turns to face her in the dark, still crouched down on the ground.

"Hana? Hana, what are you doing here? You shouldn't be out alone. C'mere," she says, and holds out her arms for the little girl to crawl into. Her voice is hoarse and thick with tears, but she manages a watery smile.

Hana comes close and sits in Mariam's lap. She puts her hands on either side of Mariam's face, rubbing her little palms over Mariam's wet cheeks.

"You're crying," she says, wonderment on her face. "Why are you crying? Are you sad?"

Mariam's first instinct is to lie—to say, no, she's not sad, everything is okay, Hana. Because isn't that what you do? Isn't that what you do when things get too hard? But Hana's looking at her with those big brown eyes and her mouth is puckered in the tiniest frown, so instead, Mariam's breath hitches with another sob and she says, "Yeah, baby. I'm sad."

Hana nods and wraps her arms around Mariam's neck. She nuzzles her face into Mariam's and gives her a wet kiss on the cheek. "Do you wanna talk about it? Sometimes I don't wanna talk about it when I'm sad, but Eomma says talking can make it better."

"Nah, I don't really want to talk about it," Mariam says, and holds Hana close. "Thanks for coming to see me, though. You're sweet, you know that?"

"I know." Hana giggles and it starts something in Mariam, too, a little spark that maybe feels like happiness in the middle of all her hurt.

She lets Hana hug her for a while longer until she stops crying and her breathing goes calm and steady. The little girl in her lap doesn't squirm or fidget, just holds her, like Mariam is the child and Hana's the grown one, and maybe that's the truth right now. She doesn't feel very grown-up at all.

Eventually, she leans back and kisses Hana on the forehead. "Hey, Hana. Let's head back home, yeah? I bet your mom's worried sick."

It's true. As soon as Mariam emerges into the firelight with Hana half asleep in her arms, Eun-Ji runs forward to snatch the child away, and Mariam can't blame her. There's accusation, but also thanks in Eun-Ji's gaze, and they both let the moment pass without words. It's easier that way.

Chapter Eighteen

ON THE SEVENTH morning since Alberich's ultimatum, Mariam wakes with the knowledge she may never open her eyes to the dim, filtered sunlight of the cave again. Or of any sunlight, for that matter, dim, filtered or otherwise. If this goes wrong, then that's it. She's dead.

She's tried to make the most of her week, spending as much time with Camila as possible, and avoiding Eun-Ji. The kids have been great, and Ishmael's been his usual smiley self, but Eun-Ji's suspicion hasn't let up, and it's been exhausting. Harder though is being party to the group's discussions on what to do next—how to get out of the jungle if it's possible. How to build a more permanent shelter. How to defend the one they have. All good things, necessary things, but talk of the future turns Mariam into a shivery mess and she ducks out as often as she can.

Camila is still asleep, murmuring her dreams out loud. Mariam should say goodbye, she figures, but...but what? Doesn't Camila deserve an actual goodbye? Probably. But if all goes well, she'll be back, in triumph, not too long from now. And if not, then, well, it doesn't really matter, does it?

Mariam creeps away from their bedroll as softly as possible.

As she's pulling on her shoes and a small voice calls out.

"Mariam?"

It's Carlos.

"Hey, buddy. Let's be quiet, yeah? We don't wanna wake anyone up."

Carlos nods somberly.

"What's up, Carlos?"

"Where are you going?'

"Oh, um. Just to get us some firewood. Get the morning going, you know."

Carlos wriggles out of his blankets, suddenly awake. "Can I come?" he asks in a mock whisper. Surely loud enough to wake Camila if she weren't so sunk in a dream.

Carlos is already stepping into his little boots, but Mariam puts a hand on his shoulder and kneels down to stop him.

"Actually, can you do me a favor, Carlos? See, everybody's still sleeping, and I don't want to leave them here without someone to guard them. Can you keep them safe this morning? I know you can do a good job."

Carlos almost protests, but soon his chest puffs up with the compliment and he nods. "I'll do such a good job. I'll watch everybody."

The image of Carlos peering at everyone while they sleep through those big glasses of his forces a smile onto her face.

"Good, thanks, kid," she says. "I knew I could count on you. Just sit here, all right? I'll be ba—just keep watch for me. Just keep watch."

Outside, the morning looks like every other morning in this place, which seems a little unfair. The Beast could have pulled out a few extra stops for her, or something. Amped up the beauty of the sunrise or made the dewdrops glisten just a little bit more. Now that she's out here, though, perhaps starting up the fire wouldn't be such a bad idea. Get them all off to a good start and all that.

But they won't need it, will they? The forest should be gone, and she should be back before they realize what she's done. Right?

Right, if she can keep her nerve. Right, if her dad, so far sunk down the path to...whatever he's become, shows up. Right, if the Beast keeps his word.

Before she realizes what she's doing, she finds her feet flying one in front of the other, pounding on the soft, mossy floor. She runs and runs until she can't run anymore, like she has her whole life, and at the end of it, she finds the Beast.

SHE COLLAPSES FROM exhaustion just far enough from the camp that maybe no one will find her body right away, but the Beast is here—she can feel It even before the smell overwhelms her, seeping through her nostrils and stinging her eyes. Mariam gulps deep breaths of the humid air, all but masking the voices that sigh through the still air.

Are you quite finished yet?

She doesn't need to look up. She knows what's there. She knows what It wants. But not yet. She's not ready. She needs...something.

"Will they see my body?" she asks, and her voice sounds blank and small even to her own ears.

It chuckles, or something like it. *The forest will take it if you wish.*

She doesn't answer, just looks at the scuffed toes of her shoes. She braces herself, then stands. The action brings sensation back to her numbed limbs, and cold washes from the crown of her head all the way down to those mud-spattered Chuck Taylors. There it is, there's the fear. It sends a trembling through her every nerve and it takes all the courage she's ever had to look up into the Beast's decay-riddled face. A smile with too many teeth is there to greet her.

Mariam breathes. In. Out. A stuttering, shaky breath, but it'll be one of her last ones, so she savors it, tastes the soft, green sunlight on her tongue past the decay surrounding her. It's enough.

"Okay. How do we do this?" she asks. She's proud that her voice stays level, but every other inch of her is quivering.

Shake my hand, child. We must seal the deal. It reaches out, extending Its bony arm toward her. The flesh is fairly dripping off of Its fingers.

Mariam takes the slightest step back. Just a step, a half-step. She has to be sure. "All right," she says, and eyes the proffered hand. "Just to be clear, if—when my dad comes to save me, he'll have to bind himself, and then all this will go away? The city will be back to normal?"

In a sense.

It's odd wording, and Mariam is about to question it when there's a rustle, a slick slither, and something different wafts through the pervasive smell of death. Cologne, sharp and spicy. Her father's footsteps make no sound on the moss.

"Mariam, step away from him," Malik says. That odd shiver in his voice is still there, but underneath it, she thinks there's a shadow of his old self too—desperate and frightened. Vulnerable: the same voice he used to plead with her to take the Beast's hand the first time.

She sees red. It's his fault. Everything is his fault. The world ending, the first plan not working, and now he has the audacity to tell her to step away from the only thing guaranteeing her friends' safety?

"Back off, Dad." She turns her face away to ask the Beast her question when her father's hand grips her shoulder. And that's it.

"Let go of me!" she yells, twisting to free herself from his grasp. Anger overwhelms her fear and she steps toward the Beast.

Mariam strikes her hand out, and the Beast takes it in a motion so fast that she can't even see. Her palm touches cold, slippery flesh and the sharp jut of knucklebones. The deal is made.

She hears her father's scream of anguish before a rushing fills her ears, and then she's the one screaming, because there's pain, now, worse than breaking her hand on the wall for Camila, worse than losing her arm, and worse than growing it back. There's lightning in her veins and her skin crackles with the heat of it. Vegetable rot suffuses her senses. She's choking.

Mariam screams and the sound of it mixes with the cacophony of voices in her head. They're speaking unspeakable words on unspeakable tongues and it's so— it's so—

The last coherent thought she has is that It's laughing at her. Laughing, with Its horrible mouth split wide and Its putrid gray tongue lolling out of a gap in the flesh of Its cheek. Laughing, and oh, that can't be a good sign. Her vision clouds over and then there's just—

Silence.

Chapter Nineteen

TIME PASSES, FULL of quiet and dark. There's no telling how long it lasts, but eventually, Mariam becomes aware of familiar sounds: the forest at night, with its crickets and mysterious clicks. She twitches her fingers to find she can move them.

It doesn't hurt anymore. At least there's that. Mariam opens her eyes to find pale, gray darkness like the night in the forest and humidity pressing down on her skin, clogging her pores, no breeze to lessen the oppressive heat. She picks herself up unsteadily, joints complaining like she's been lying here for ages and ages with moss growing into her hair.

She stands, brushes the leaves off her jeans, and begins walking.

If this is hell, it isn't too different from the world she's become used to, she realizes, making her way through the undergrowth. The trees, the vines, the moss. The chittering and slithering of things just out of sight. It's familiar enough, except for the people. At first, she doesn't notice them, but as she walks on, she begins to see human forms nestled in the vegetation: hundreds and hundreds of them, huddled up in fetal positions and crying, gnashing their teeth. Their moans sound like the creaking of ancient trees. Then there are others, standing or sitting, glowing, moving their mouths, soundlessly speaking to each other as though they don't see the hundreds of suffering people lying at their feet.

She walks on, and on, and on.

None of them turns to look at her as she passes, and she feels a curious disinterest in them as well. She starts to recognize people, but even these arouse only the slightest curiosity in her. A teacher of hers that died of leukemia when she was little. The aunt she knows only from pictures. She doesn't stop to say hello.

She's been walking for hours, it seems, through a never-ending hall of trees when suddenly, to her left, she hears a woman's voice, the first human voice she's heard since she's been here, and the sound of it intrigues her. She turns away from the path and wanders through the trees until she finds a middle-aged couple sitting on mossy rocks in the middle of a clearing. It takes her a moment to recognize them, but when she does, something keen and desperate bursts in her. Her grandparents passed a few years after her mother when she had been twelve. And there they are: sitting on those rocks as if they were rocking chairs and conversing just the way they used to when she was younger. They died horrifically in a car accident, but here they look fine, better than they ever did. Their glow is easy to see in the darkness, and the moment they catch sight of her is obvious because their faces light up with genuine joy.

Mariam almost tears up, calls out, tentative, "Teta? Gedo?"

"Mariam!" Her grandmother cries, pulling her into an embrace. "Alhamdulillah, you are here in paradise!"

"Teta," Mariam breathes and buries her face in her grandmother's perfumed neck. It smells like home, and it's wonderful, and oh God. Her grandparents would be horrified to learn that their eldest son is next in line to become the ruler of hell or whatever this place is.

Then she processes her grandmother's words and stills. Teta said paradise. Not that Mariam is an expert on the various degrees of the afterlife, but this place sure doesn't look like paradise. "What...Teta, I don't understand. Paradise?"

"We knew you would convert, even if your father left the faith. You were always such a good girl, listening to me and Gedo when we told you the stories. Such a good girl." There's a tremor in the dark, and her grandmother says again, "Such a good girl." The ground beneath them shakes, and the trees groan as their trunks sway. Teta and Gedo are fading into the darkness, her grandmother's arms around her neck disintegrating until even the glow is gone.

Mariam stands still, shocked, until she starts calling for her grandparents. She stays for what feels like hours, until her throat starts to hurt, but it becomes obvious they aren't coming back. She's alone again, and it's somehow worse this time.

Eventually, she walks on, stumbling every now and then as the ground rumbles beneath her. The trace of a path she'd been following has disappeared. There's no sense of direction here, not even the suggestion of moonlight to guide her, just trees and trees and trees and the anguish of the people tangled in their roots.

She walks until she hears someone singing, the only song from her childhood she can remember, from before her mom killed herself.

It's nice, almost comforting, she thinks, until she realizes the voice is familiar. It sounds like...like Mom? She doesn't dare to hope, but already her feet are lifting, and she runs through the forest toward the sound. She's reaching for her hatchet to hack her way through a thick bundle of vines when she realizes: it's not there. Her hatchet, it's gone.

Mariam pauses for a moment, but the song becomes louder, and it's clear that it's coming from the other side of this tangle of vines. She begins to go at the vines with her bare hands, but it burns, God it burns, and she isn't healing.

She keeps going, because what, really, will burned palms matter in the grand scheme of things? She'll be here forever if she understands rightly. Daddy would've been here by now if he were coming at all, and that's her mother's voice on the other side, she's sure of it now. She's so close.

The last of the vines fall away under her hands, and she steps through. It's no different on this side, just more trees fading away into thick darkness on every side, briars and vines catching at her legs. But there: there's the voice, and Mariam trips forward toward it. She rounds a moss-furred trunk and stops, reeling.

There's a woman sitting at the base of the tree, her face turned away. Her clothes are disheveled and her blond hair falls lank around her ears, but that's the thing. It's her blond hair. They're her ears. It's her. It's her mother. It's Mama.

She doesn't have the same glow her grandparents did, but she's singing that song, the same one. Mariam doesn't know what to say. What should she say? What would she have wanted to say at six years old if she'd found something different behind the study door? She doesn't know, so instead, she sings along.

Her voice is wavering at first, but as it picks up in strength, her mother starts at the unexpected accompaniment. Mama doesn't stop singing, just turns quick to look at Mariam. There's a split second during which Mariam's stomach drops out and she expects to see the Beast's face there like in all her dreams, but it isn't. It's her mother's face, and her mother's eyes, and her mother's smiling mouth forming the words to this song Mariam never thought she'd hear again from any lips but her own.

"Mama," she says and collapses down to her knees to throw her arms around her mother's neck.

The song falters, and then there are hands pushing her away.

"I'm sorry, I—I think you've mistaken me for someone else..." Her mother says and leans away. In her eyes, there's confusion, maybe a little bit of alarm.

Mariam's hands grab at her mother's sleeves, fingers twisting in the fabric. "No, no, Mom, it's me. It's me, Mariam. Don't you...? Don't you know me? I—" She stumbles over her words, pauses and swallows. "I know I'm older, but it's me. I'm your daughter. I'm your daughter; you're my mom."

Her mother shakes her head. "No, I'm sorry. My daughter is six years old. She's asleep in the other room right now, you can see for yourself."

Mariam looks and there's nothing, nothing but the rainforest, probably for miles. Probably forever.

"No..." She lets go of her mother's sleeves and shuffles back on her knees. Her hands are shaking, her voice too. "You really don't know me?"

There's no recognition in her mother's gaze. Just blank, blue eyes.

She almost cries out but claps a hand over her mouth and stumbles to her feet instead. She has to go. She has to leave this place. She runs, tripping and getting her feet tangled in vines and scraping her hands on rough bark as the ground shifts beneath her. The forest goes on, and on, and on.

Behind every tree, there's a voice, and over and over again Mariam finds herself confronted with that blank stare, singing a lullaby that's not meant for her.

It takes a while, but eventually, it hits her. There is no leaving this place. This is it. This is forever.

Her knees buckle, and she lets herself fall heavy onto the moss. She curls in on herself, mimicking the bodies all around her, mimicking their sobbing, too. It's not even like any of this was worth it, because Dad's not coming for her, and the others are still stuck in that hell-jungle, and she's here, and she's all alone.

She feels small, a tiny curl of blood and flesh in a vast jungle. Though is it, really, blood and flesh still? What is she made of in this place? Her stinging palms say that she's alive, but she's not. She's dead, dead, dead, and she'll be dead for the rest of forever.

She feels small, and then suddenly she is small, she's six years old and that's not moss under her cheek; it's carpet. Carpet, and not far from her nose, the wood of the study door. Behind her, she knows, is her mother, not singing this time, but sprawled on the floor, dead too, her life leaking out into her hair.

She doesn't know how long she stays there, crying on the floor. It feels like an eternity. But then the door swings open and two polished shoes step in front of her face. Two arms reach down to pick her up off the floor, lift her into the air. Cologne, sharp and spicy.

"Don't cry, Mariam. It's okay. Daddy's got you," her father's voice says, and his hand strokes her hair.

He turns and carries her out of the study. The door shuts behind them.

Fifth Interlude

HE REALLY WAS planning to watch them, like Mariam said, honest. And at first, he did, sitting cross-legged on top of his blankets, surveying the dim cave and making sure every sleeping lump stayed a sleeping lump.

But an adventure! With Mariam! In the morning time! Carlos's squirms had grown bigger and bigger, and eventually, he had given in. He'd pulled on his boots and scooted over to Hana's blanket nest, poking the girl in the cheek until her brow furrowed and she woke.

"Ssh! Hana, okay, I need you to do something. Watch the people. Mariam says it's important. Watch the people."

Hana yawned and half turned over. "Okay, Carlos," she murmured, eyes closed.

Carlos sat back on his heels, considering. Well, he tried, right?

So now he's crashing through the forest, leaping over branches and vines, surprising clouds of green butterflies into flight. Mariam is easy to follow: her hatchet isn't very subtle, and Ishmael's taught Carlos a few things about tracking. He's a pro, now.

Still, she's farther from the camp than Carlos is used to, and he's curious. Eun-Ji says Mariam isn't what she seems and that Hana and Carlos need to be careful. Carlos doesn't know what she means by that. It's not like Mariam's ever hit him, not like—but then, Carlos doesn't like to think of his last foster parents. Besides, Mariam's nothing like the Grahams were. She only hurts things that are scary, and she's always nice to him. He likes her.

He arrives just in time to hear Mariam scream.

A monster hovers over her, tall and white. Mariam's body stiffens, twists, and then goes still. The monster makes a terrible sound, like laughter if laughter were the worst thing in the world. Carlos shrinks behind a large sticky leaf. Not far from him, the monster moves, talking maybe, but Carlos's brain is whirring too fast to make sense of it. Carlos is brave. Braver than most. Braver than is smart, or prudent, or useful, sometimes. But something deep in Carlos' seven-year-old bones tells him that now is not the time to be brave, so he turns, and runs. This is a job for grown-ups.

He barrels into the cave, boots slapping at the concrete floor, and leaps into Camila's arms.

Before she can ask what's wrong, the words are tumbling from his mouth. "There's a monster. And Mariam. And she fell down and it smelled so bad and it laughed."

Camila grabs Carlos by the shoulders, and it scares him, the urgency in her eyes, but not as much as that monster did.

"Carlos. Slow down. What happened? Tell me."

By now Carlos is crying, hiccupping and sobbing between every word, face buried in Camila's shoulder.

"I followed Mariam and there was a big monster, and I think it got her, Camila. Please get Ishmael. I think she's dead; I think she's dead."

Chapter Twenty

HER HEAD IS pounding; someone is forcing air into her lungs. She coughs, and the smell of rot fills her nostrils. She can feel Its presence, but the light behind her eyelids is brightening, brightening.

Someone shouts, "She's breathing!" and someone, maybe the same person, is squeezing her hand.

She wills her eyes open, just a crack. The light almost blinds her, but after a moment she makes out the blurry shapes of the people around her. Her father is standing with his back to her, missing his dark suit coat, shirt disheveled. He says something, but she can't make it out through the ringing in her ears.

She blinks to clear her vision and realizes the Beast is there as well, Its great white figure hulking against the filtered sunlight.

Its voice, invasive and choral as ever, rings through the damp air, into her skull.

She wakes, It says, and within moments she feels her father's breath on her face, his tears dripping warm onto her cheeks.

She wakes, and now you must fulfill your end of the bargain. Fulfill your vow, Malik. My patience is at its end.

Mariam watches her father rise to his feet, straighten his tie, and tug on the cuffs of his sleeves. He steps over to the Beast and makes a strange salute. Her father's voice is amplified even through his tears and so when he says, "I, Malik Aboul-Nour, will become caretaker of the Realm of the Dead, until such a time as a suitable successor can be found."

She hears every word. He continues speaking, this time in the language Mariam recognizes from his rituals, a sonorous, rhythmic chant that resonates in her head like the voice of the Beast.

Finally, the Beast says, and laughs and laughs and laughs.

The earth begins to tremble, and the light grows too strong for Mariam's newly opened eyes. She can hear Hana whimpering, something about the trees shrinking, and someone is clutching her hand so hard it hurts. The ground's tremble intensifies into a shudder, then into a shaking so violent she feels it in her bones. It doesn't stop, not for what feels like forever. From all around her, a slithering, crackling, creaking sound joins the rumbling of the earth.

It stops more suddenly than it began. Mariam wants to open her eyes again, to see what all that fuss was about, but they're so heavy. It's too much, for now. This time when she falls, it's not into the hell-jungle, but unconsciousness. Dreamless, quiet sleep.

WHEN SHE FINALLY awakes, her eyesight is still blurry, but the first thing she notices is that it's as bright as it gets down by the riverbank. The second thing she notices is that she can't hear the sound of rushing water, but those two things don't add up. Neither does the fact that she's here, to notice the light at all, but, honestly? She should stop being surprised by this stuff.

The sounds of people talking come to her as though she's underwater, but over all the others, she recognizes her father's baritone.

"...a little weak for a couple of days. She's been through a shock, and I don't think her healing is kicking in anytime soon."

"Does that mean she's not lucky anymore?" That's Carlos if she's not mistaken.

The voices go on, but she's tired, so tired. She turns to the comfort of unconsciousness again but finds that the sounds around her are getting clearer and that the light doesn't hurt her eyes so much.

"What's going on?" she manages to croak, and someone beside her jumps. When she turns to identify her skittish companion, it's Camila.

"Mariam, I swear I'm going to kill you!" Camila's face turns that lovely shade of pink, except, uh-oh, it's 'cause she's angry this time.

"Please, don't. Dying sucks," Mariam rasps and swallows slowly. Her tongue is dry, sticking to the roof of her mouth and unpleasantly thick.

She squints to get her vision to clear. There's nothing at first, just Camila's face and a blankness behind her, and then Mariam realizes that the blankness is the sky: blue and clear and not obscured by a single waving branch. She turns her head slowly, left, right. Not a tree in sight. No vines, no moss; just a concrete wall with cracks like spider veins and a concrete floor that's in the same shape, gray and stained with the remnants of some ancient spray paint.

"What happened?" Mariam asks. Her voice sounds hoarse from misuse.

"Oh God. Where do I start? You killed yourself! You gave yourself up to that—that thing, you stubborn, stubborn—"

"No, I mean—" Mariam knows there are probably more pressing things to ask about, but she can't get this question out of her head, "It promised you guys wouldn't find me like this." There's a pleading note that she can't keep out of her voice, raspy as it is. "You weren't meant to find me like this."

"Carlos."

Mariam curses. "I told him to watch you guys."

Camila closes her eyes and breathes. "This isn't his fault. He's a baby and he looks up to you, so he followed you and watched you die. And he saw Alberich." Camila explains what happened and finishes with, "I think he'd like to talk to you, but we wanted to let you rest."

"No, he can—" Mariam sits up a bit and gasps as a headache forms. She hasn't had a headache since she was six. She's forgotten what they feel like. "It's fine. It'd probably do him good to see me awake and stuff."

"Yes, it would." Camila rubs the space between her eyebrows and looks at Mariam with accusation in her gaze. "Why?"

Mariam deflates. "It said I could save you. It said my dad would come rescue me from hell and we could have everything back to normal again."

"We would've found another way!"

"No. It... it said if I didn't do this, the jungle would start attacking us again. Camila. I didn't have a choice."

"You were dead," Camila says. "Your heart stopped beating and you were dead! How do you think that will impact Carlos? How do you think it will impact me? I saw the person I love dead, and I was holding your body, your dead body, and you have no idea—"

"I have some idea, Camila."

Camila is crying, her hot tears falling on Mariam's skin. "How could you do this without telling me?"

"Because you would've talked me out of it and I'm not strong enough to say no to you. I didn't want you to have to live like this anymore. Any of you. I'm sorry, I'm really sorry Camila. But I had to do it. I didn't have a choice."

Camila is taking deep breaths, trying to quell her tears. "I'm really mad at you."

Mariam nods. "I know. And you can be mad at me. But look, no more weird trees," Mariam says, craning her stiff neck left and right to see. There's nothing, not a single vine or tree or bush. Just a concrete landscape as far as she can see, dotted with the ruins of what used to be Los Angeles. Here and there thin threads of smoke waver against the bright sky—survivors, like them.

"Yeah, I guess. I mean that's great, obviously. But Mariam—" Camila leans over to look Mariam straight in the face. "—don't you do anything stupid like that ever again."

SHE'S SEEN EVERYONE, hugged everyone, had her legs squeezed and her cheeks kissed and been presented with flower crowns and a tin of mandarins.

She's apologized to Carlos, who says, "You must be really, really lucky. Like Jesus."

Hana's still here, just curled up under her arm to keep her company as she gets her strength back. Mariam's dozing in the sun, fingers stroking absently through Hana's hair when someone clears their throat nearby. Mariam looks up to find her father standing not far away.

"Hey, Hana," she says into the little girl's ear. "How about you go keep Camila company, huh?"

Hana glances up at Malik and shivers a little, but gets to her feet and scuttles past him. Her father steps forward, awkward, and Mariam gets a good look at him for the first time since she's been back from hell.

In the sunlight, it's easier to tell he's still not quite there, blurred at the edges and humming with some sort of energy that feels alien to the living world. But his face is still her father's face. He smiles, tight, and it seems real enough.

"How's my little girl doing?" he asks.

She scowls, but she isn't sure she means it. "I'm still mad at you, you know."

"I know." He sighs and sinks down to sit on the ground next to her. "You have every right to be, I...I have made some mistakes. I only ever wanted to protect you, and even after everything, I failed. I'm sorry, Mariam."

"It's not that," she says, because it isn't. She would have forgiven him for letting her fall, for letting her get hurt, and letting her die, and even for being a terrible, terrible father. "It's...everything else. It's what you became, all the people you killed. I don't know who you are, Dad. I couldn't trust you. I still don't know if I do. You did really horrible things."

"I know," he says again. "I'm trying to make it right. I'm, well, I'm taking over the Beast's position if you haven't heard. And if I do it well, nothing like this will ever happen again."

"I hope not."

There's a moment of silence between them. Mariam can hear Hana and Carlos shouting further away, laughing like children should.

Laughing, like they don't have a care in the world. Soon they won't be alone here anymore. Now that the jungle is gone, it'll only be matter of time before help arrives. Mariam is glad for it, but something is bothering her. Something feels off. It comes to her then, a shudder at the thought of all those people in the trees, their teeth chattering as they relive their worst fears forever and forever. It didn't seem fair.

"Is that how it really is?" She asks. "The Realm of the Dead, is it really so..."

Malik frowns and gives a little shudder himself, as though he too remembers the pervasive damp and the incessant droning of the dead.

"No, I...I don't think so. I think that was my doing," he says. "Something came loose—off balance—when I didn't do my job. There was no one to take care of it all, so it...deteriorated."

"It was...it was so sad, Daddy. I saw... I saw Mom. She didn't know who I was. She didn't know I was her kid."

Malik shakes his head. "I think what you saw was part of it coming loose. Your mother, she's fine. And she knows who you are, love. She would never forget you."

They sit in silence for a moment, before her father clears his throat again. "I'll be leaving soon."

"Will I get to see you again?" It's suddenly urgent, suddenly imperative, that she does. She doesn't know when she started to need her father again, as twisted as he may be, but she certainly does now. Her fingers twitch to reach for his hand.

"I don't know," he says. "There is a lot of work to be done. Stewarding the Realm of the Dead will be a demanding task, and there are limitations on what I can do. Where I can go. So..." He looks at her with a suggestion of love in his eyes, and Mariam would swear he's tearing up. "...so this might be goodbye, for now."

She does reach up, then, to wrap her arms around his neck and breathe in his scent, both familiar and so very wrong. He hugs her back, for the first time in years, perhaps. She wants to ask him to stay, but she knows she can't.

"You have good friends, here," he murmurs into her ear. "They'll take care of you for me."

Tears blur her eyesight as he releases her from the embrace, and she watches him walk away.

At Hana's seventh birthday party, Mariam dodges between the Mulan-themed streamers that festoon the ceiling and walls. Her head brushes against a few as she strides into Eun-Ji's bright kitchen.

Camila's voice shouts through the din behind her, "...and don't forget the pizza cutter! This place never cuts it right!"

Mariam laughs to herself and rifles through the drawers, procuring napkins and said pizza cutter.

She's making her way through the crowd when one of Hana's innumerable friends comes careening around the corner and collides with her knees. She goes stumbling against the wall, biting back a bad word for the children's sake. The pizza cutter in her hands, though dull, slices into her skin, and ow, that hurts.

Camila comes through the crowd to help, and finds Mariam laughing at the blood seeping down the lines of her palm.

The cut isn't healing.

Camila scolds her, but the grin on Mariam's face lasts all evening. Nearly two years and she still hasn't gotten over the novelty of healing up on her own time.

"Go get a Band-Aid, you weirdo. I'll take care of this," Camila says, gathering up the napkins and bloody pizza cutter.

In the bathroom, Mariam rinses off the cut and applies some ointment and a Band-Aid from Eun-Ji's extensive first aid kit. She overstocks on all kinds of emergency supplies, and Mariam doesn't blame her. It's part of how Eun-Ji copes with everything. Even now, in their new home hundreds and hundreds of miles from LA, she gets the feeling that none of them can keep the jungle out of their thoughts for long. The press still churns up conspiracy theories about what happened there, now and then, but even though the few survivors have offered up enough bizarre stories to fuel cryptid legends of a man in a suit for years, no one has ever been able to explain how a rainforest popped up in the middle of the desert for half a year.

Well, Mariam could. Eun-Ji could. Camila, Ishmael, Luci, and even Hana and Carlos could. But Eun-Ji's never let anyone get close enough to ask, and they like it that way.

By the time Mariam gets back, Eun-Ji's handing out slices of pizza to a horde of shrieking children, whose faces are already smeared with crumbs and the colorful evidence of gummy bears. It's chaos, but there's Hana, standing on one of the chairs in her favorite blue dress, holding court over the throng. Carlos is behind her, acting every bit the responsible older brother and making sure everyone receives their obligatory napkin.

Mariam waves at them from the doorway and receives two beaming grins in return. If she looks close, she can still see the criss-crossing scars on Carlos's arms, but only just.

Luci is around somewhere, probably sulking in adolescent gloom. She'll be in later, Mariam guesses, to steal some pizza and a slice of cake or two.

"Pizza, Mariam?" Ishmael sidles up beside her in the doorway, holding out a greasy slice on a paper plate.

"Thanks, Ishmael," she says.

As she observes the children, Camila comes over to put her head on Mariam's shoulder and tap the back of her hand.

"Did you disinfect it?" she asks, stern.

"Yes." Mariam sighs. Camila still won't let her forget the infected cut that landed Mariam in the hospital last year. Mariam still maintains she can't be expected to know much about first aid, but they've agreed to disagree.

"Good."

And as always, Camila's faux-frown crooks into a smile and she rises up on her toes to kiss Mariam's cheek.

Epilogue

AT HANA'S SEVENTH birthday party, Mariam dodges between the Mulan-themed streamers that festoon the ceiling and walls. Her head brushes against a few as she strides into Eun-Ji's bright kitchen.

Camila's voice shouts through the din behind her, "...and don't forget the pizza cutter! This place never cuts it right!"

Mariam laughs to herself and rifles through the drawers, procuring napkins and said pizza cutter.

She's making her way through the crowd when one of Hana's innumerable friends comes careening around the corner and collides with her knees. She goes stumbling against the wall, biting back a bad word for the children's sake. The pizza cutter in her hands, though dull, slices into her skin, and ow, that hurts.

Camila comes through the crowd to help, and finds Mariam laughing at the blood seeping down the lines of her palm.

The cut isn't healing.

Camila scolds her, but the grin on Mariam's face lasts all evening. Nearly two years and she still hasn't gotten over the novelty of healing up on her own time.

"Go get a Band-Aid, you weirdo. I'll take care of this," Camila says, gathering up the napkins and bloody pizza cutter.

In the bathroom, Mariam rinses off the cut and applies some ointment and a Band-Aid from Eun-Ji's extensive first aid kit. She overstocks on all kinds of emergency supplies, and Mariam doesn't blame her. It's part of how Eun-Ji copes with everything. Even now, in their new home hundreds and hundreds of miles from LA, she gets the feeling that none of them can keep the jungle out of their thoughts for long. The press still churns up conspiracy theories about what happened there, now and then, but even though the few survivors have offered up enough bizarre stories to fuel cryptid legends of a man in a suit for years, no one has ever been able to explain how a rainforest popped up in the middle of the desert for half a year.

Well, Mariam could. Eun-Ji could. Camila, Ishmael, Luci, and even Hana and Carlos could. But Eun-Ji's never let anyone get close enough to ask, and they like it that way.

By the time Mariam gets back, Eun-Ji's handing out slices of pizza to a horde of shrieking children, whose faces are already smeared with crumbs and the colorful evidence of gummy bears. It's chaos, but there's Hana, standing on one of the chairs in her favorite blue dress, holding court over the throng. Carlos is behind her, acting every bit the responsible older brother and making sure everyone receives their obligatory napkin.

Mariam waves at them from the doorway and receives two beaming grins in return. If she looks close, she can still see the criss-crossing scars on Carlos's arms, but only just.

Luci is around somewhere, probably sulking in adolescent gloom. She'll be in later, Mariam guesses, to steal some pizza and a slice of cake or two.

"Pizza, Mariam?" Ishmael sidles up beside her in the doorway, holding out a greasy slice on a paper plate.

"Thanks, Ishmael," she says.

As she observes the children, Camila comes over to put her head on Mariam's shoulder and tap the back of her hand.

"Did you disinfect it?" she asks, stern.

"Yes." Mariam sighs. Camila still won't let her forget the infected cut that landed Mariam in the hospital last year. Mariam still maintains she can't be expected to know much about first aid, but they've agreed to disagree.

"Good."

And as always, Camila's faux-frown crooks into a smile and she rises up on her toes to kiss Mariam's cheek.

Acknowledgements

Thanks to Chel's wife, Bee, and Chelsea's partner, Nicholas, for their support throughout the writing process.

Thanks to Mallory for helping with Hana's story, and Fadwa and Magie for their sensitivity reading.

Thank you, Rivers, for their insight into the publishing world.

Thank you, Sam, for being a wonderfully insightful editor.

And thank you to countless other friends and family whose support made this story possible.

About the Authors

Chel Hylott lives in Surrey, England with her wife and her dog. When she's not writing, she's reading Tarot or listening to 70s Brazilian music.

Chelsea Lim is a writer and teacher living in Los Angeles, which she almost wishes were as green as it is in Undergrowth.

Email: ChelandChels@gmail.com

Twitter: @actuallychel, @lim_chels

Also Available from NineStar Press

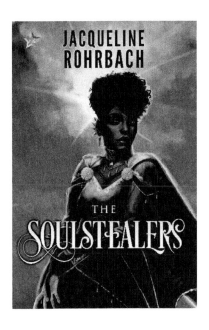

Connect with NineStar Press

www.ninestarpress.com

www.facebook.com/ninestarpress

www.facebook.com/groups/NineStarNiche

www.twitter.com/ninestarpress

www.tumblr.com/blog/ninestarpress

Printed in Great Britain
by Amazon

46764075R00128